A
Term of
Existence

A Collection
of Verse

Ken Mann

First published in 2016 by Ken Mann, Brisbane, Qld, Australia.

ISBN 978-0-9942598-6-8 (eBook)
ISBN 978-0-9942598-7-5 (eBook)
ISBN 978-0-9942598-4-4 (softback)
ISBN 978-0-9942598-5-1 (softback)

This is a work of fiction. All characters and events depicted in these pages are products of the author's imagination, and any similarity to actual persons or events is unintended and coincidental.

For further information,
you may contact me via the following channels;

www.kenmann.net

or follow me on Facebook at;

www.facebook.com/kenmannauthor

I am grateful to the following services that
assisted me in getting this novel to publication;

Cover Design;
Created by Ken Mann – credit is given to the following Dreamstime
artists whose works contributed to the final cover;
Unholyvault

Editorial Services;
Elderberry Press Australia

Formatting;
Ken Mann

For Jane, Rachel, Natasha, Tristan, Lorelei & Aidan and all those who have influenced my work over the many years that I've been writing poetry including my parents and those who've found themselves the subjects of some of my work.

<u>About the Author</u>

As long as I have known him, Ken has preferred to use alternative forms of communication to express his feelings. In fact, Ken has an ability to express his every emotion. For those of us who know the 'real' Ken (and I am sure through reading his work, you will receive an insight into the man), would class him as the all original sensitive new age guy. This trait was obvious well before this became the "adopted" male attitude of the late 80's early 90's.

"Live Each Day As If It Were Your Last". Most of us dream about living one day like this. Since we were very young, Ken has had the enviable ability to live like this every day. This sort of living takes a lot of energy. This amount of energy can only come from someone who is out chasing their dream. I am not trying to paint Ken as a Superman or a Saint. However, he does have a quality as rare today as sainthood. The ability to dream. This gift on its own is not enough. Ken also has the courage to sell out to his dream, chase it down and make it happen. This work is a product of that dream.

Together at school, we dabbled in the written form of expression. Me, simply because I had to, for assessment. Ken's natural flair soon became evident. The work before you is a natural progression from these early days as a spirited student to the accomplished, polished artist that is Ken Mann.

Justin Hart…

<u>Preface</u>

Poetry is essentially a rhythmic art form/story constructed from the inner thoughts of a writer, the poet. Yet nearly every poet that one reads, alters to some degree our total perception of poetry. To me as a writer, it is an expression of beautiful or elevated thought, imagination or feelings that are used in appropriate language.

I myself tend to prefer to call poetry, verse. But it is how verse originated that interested me in some recent research. It is said that it is most probable that verse (poetry) originated in the magical spells, ritualistic incantations, and the highly rhythmical and formalised storytelling of early tribal society.

Even in its periods of greatest religious and magical significance, it seems to have been regarded as a game to be played with words. Similar to Limericks which originated in Ireland. It was a form of entertainment, a pastime, and an outlet for one to convey an emotional release. It was also used as a form of communication for religious-political ceremonials. In the modern age of literature, some of these purposes as in the beginning still hold the same values, although verse is changing to suit the changing times.

Writing verse is an escape route from all present surroundings, knowing that your mind is locked onto the one subject. Engaging this style of writing with no outside source of distraction can thrust upon you many emotions that rarely disclose themselves in the everyday environment.

My philosophy is that everything has a perfect match. Magnets are governed by either north or south poles, two norths will detract and so will two souths. Two opposites have to be used in conjunction with a match, thus opposites attract. Unless in a situation as this, the chemistry for success is missing. Two halves make a whole and twenty-three plus twenty-three chromosomes form an embryo giving life to a new creation.

This goes hand in hand with writing, to excel in this and other fields, the barriers of limitations, censorship's, and pressures have to be shut out when the mind enters a state of total self-confession and expression.

My early verses were plain. They still contained standard rhythmic patterns, though they lacked Poetic Imagery, Similes, Metaphors, and Symbols. These elements are an essential ingredient for broadening views and perspective of ideologies.

After introducing this format to my writing, I believe that the depth and meaning of the message behind the verse will make the reader stop and think. I have tried to place a moral issue behind most of my verses. Some are hard-line and straight forward, which in the subject that they are representing, highlight the need for awareness and immediate attention. The others still have a hidden message but they have been designed to make the reader think just that little more.

My belief is that we were all created for a reason whether that be a doctor, labourer, or a corner store salesman. Each and every one of us was created to serve each other. One aspires to be an example and to make even the person next to you admire your skills and talents. Every occupation and job skill serves and benefits another human being. So one's destiny has to be chosen very carefully. I enjoy writing simply for the thrill of creation and accomplishment, not as an extra income nor a second occupation. Very few if any can survive only due to this form of writing. Though verse has created its own destiny and place in our society, not a large percentage of a population would ever indulge in writing a verse outside their adolescent scholastic careers.

I am naturally a quiet person and I don't usually voice an opinion on a subject unless I am in a raged mood, although this is changing with age. Therefore, I find that verse is a suitable alternative. I can say exactly what I want to say, how I say it and shape it into a direct to the point structure that people will take notice of, without the annoying interruptions. Government officials and Public speakers try the same concept and never succeed, and that's how they're remembered.

I write on a number of subjects and one particular one is romance. What is love? Everybody seems to have their own meaning towards describing the emotion. It is said in the bible (so I am told) that one must love thyself before one can love another. Some people may hear this and shrug the idea off and display ridicule. But, seriously think about it, if you don't like something about yourself, then you will be lacking in self-confidence. This will, in turn, affect your ego or your feelings. With this in mind, you will not be able to make yourself comfortable when you're approaching or interacting with the opposite sex or potentially in any social environment.

Writers portray love and romance more than often in a fictional sense or otherwise we would be the greatest lovers in the world. It's more than often an escape into mind, mixing thought with sexual desire. Creating scenes of tables being waited, cocktails stirring, beautiful young women, naked bodies, soft breezes, drifting curtains, and music that gently breaks the silence. These shape the mood and structure to support the message the writer is trying to convey.

I think modern writers have strayed away from the classic love tale of yesteryear due to the more liberal sexual and moral standards of today's society. People, in my opinion, get bored of traditional literature and are searching for more modern forms of entertainment. I don't mean that all moral standards are forgotten but that people accept the changes of writing standards as time changes the way we live. Another subject that I write about is war. War and human conflict has over many centuries back to the birth of mankind, captivated the imagination of all. Especially the likes of Napoleon, Nelson and others. It may not be the topic that all want to read, and most would not want to glorify such tragedies however I believe that writing about this subject is not glorifying but celebrating an aspect of human triumph in the face of extreme adversity regardless of the result. But in future, one can hope that world peace draws nearer with each day. With this in mind, war should be documented in all forms of media to remind us all of the human loss and sufferings that this barbarism inflicts.

In my writing about the subject, I have tried to point towards the misery and pain. My belief is that documentation to remind us is a deterrent if only everyone believed this! My other work touches on issues that are current to the time such as animal rights. Others are solely to entertain and a mix of verses that portray the hardships of growing in today's society.

Verse is not just a form of writing that rhymes, it's an art form that thrives on perfection. Close your eyes and imagine a page of writing before you. It's not a song and it's not a novel or short story. It may portray the grace of the ballet, a young soldier slowly dying on the battlefield, white palm-draped beaches, beautiful women or evil phenomena. What you have just imagined is probably the groundwork for a masterpiece of verse. Think, your mind was concentrating on one subject. You placed yourself in the scene and your mind was flowing in descriptive thought. The only thing missing is the pen and paper (word processor maybe) and a relevant sentence structure to present your idea. That is verse in its entire context. Verse is eighty percent based on non-fictional events or places as well as their characters. That means that every piece of verse that you read is part of living history. Not only in the real sense of the meaning but that you are finding out the personal thoughts of a human being at the time it was written. Living thought and memory.

We are the unspoken truth tellers of the world. We portray the truth and the message on subjects that need addressing but with the purpose to entertain.

Author's Note...

I'd like to open by saying that without the input, encouragement and at times, moments of self-pity and discontentment, I would not have been able to write these verses or for a better term, I would not have cared to put my feelings and thoughts on paper. The credit of this encouragement goes to the people that I have named in my acknowledgements or written about. The other, my self-pity and discontentment are mainly due to the thoughts and feelings that one feels when fate throws one's self into a situation that at that particular time, makes us ponder whether life could get any worse.

As far as a timeline is concerned, this collection was originally written between 1987 and 2010. Many others were not been included as I didn't feel that they were relevant for the purposes of the collection for various reasons. My scope of subject covers many true, fictitious, and bizarre verses as well as personal accounts in my life. You will also note a change of writing style and complexity from my early to latter verses as I grew in both maturity and experience. I did not however arrange the format of this collection in chronological order. Let me say at this point, the Kelran series is an unfinished piece of work, one that I will transform into an epic fantasy novel (not associated with The Wiccan Tales series) and secondly the verse "The Perfect Masterpiece". It is simply the latter, a replication of the verse "A Masterpiece" written in an obscure font. Did you think it was a foreign language verse? Don't be concerned if you did, many before you have as well. Just a little trickery☺. It may seem that I have done many things in my life to this point, to which I have and that I am proud of except I have not yet completed half of my lives ambitions and goals. I do not see working as "work rather I use working as medium or tool to finance my lives real ambitions, so no matter how good or bad work may be going, I remind myself that I have six more months before I reach the point by where I can do this or afford that, rather than look at work as forty-five years of my life to enjoy the remaining years thereafter no matter how long or short they may be.

I feel that some people who treat life this way lose its meaning. If we better ourselves while enjoying the fulfilment along the way whether they be spiritual, material or personal by breaking up the years into short-term goals rather than the one long term goal, contentment will be assured. The key to this is to pick the right moments and aim for the right goals that will make you a happier and a content member of the community.

Contact me with any questions. I'd love to hear from you. Also, leave reviews at your place of purchase as it will assist your fellow readers

Take care…

Titles Available

The Black Locust – Book 1 (The Wiccan Tales)

Endless Worlds Vol 1 Anthology (Sci-Fi, Horror & Fantasy)

Endless Worlds Vol 2 Anthology (Dark Faerie Tales)

A Term of Existence (A Collection of Selected Verse) with bonus excerpt of "The Black Locust"

Muse - Book 2 (The Wiccan Tales) - (To be released early 2017)

Contents

Forbidden Fruit

Kelran (Part 1)

Lighthouse Blues

Perplexed

Alice

A New Dawn is Born

Dionaea Muscipula

Kelran (Part 2)

A Portrait of Boredom

Secrets of the Femme Wolf

Not Yet Nineteen

An Underprivileged Psychology

Bahamas

Arena Warriors

I'm in the Front but Who's in the Back

Carmel, my Crème Caramel

Kelran (Part 3)

Love and War

Mein Feiertag

Photogenic

A Name for Life

Vampires Ghost

Illuminate Tangerine Tiger Trail

The Bottle

Strike Three….You're Out!

Belinda

Australis Australia

An Uplifting Love Affair

Karita's Nightmare

For You

Rendezvous for Lust or Escape?

Sinnliche Begierde

Solitaire Failures of Emptiness

Suburban Life – Saturday Morning Antics

The Blue and The Grey

The Long Hard Thirst

Times of the Tortured

Uneducated or Not Having An Appreciation

You're a Paradise to Me

Solicitude

A German Coin has Two Sides Too!

The Untitled Verse

The Black Forest

Something so Good

Luwunu

A Letter to Jane

A Term of Existence

The puppeteer's strings tighten,
grievance encases the soul.
Idle hours slip by so fast,
in the pursuit of the one treasured goal.

Mastery is to overcome non-fulfilment,
phenomenal resistance not to fall.
A strength in the field of diversion,
careers being nominated for recall.

Nocturnal events that silhouette the evil,
melancholia fighting for the wheel.
Striving for that elusive dollar,
for a purchase that tends to be on appeal

Vassals of synthetic organic compounds,
investments in stocks and bonds.
A joining in conjugal union,
an overload waiting to respond.

An agitated moment of confusion,
opportunities reluctant to spawn.
Regalia obtained on furlough,
anxiety while an infant is born.

Striving to adorn upon success,
walking the thin rope.
A divorce followed by a court case,
all seems to have diminished from lives hope.

A child custody battles in torment,
anguish has taken to the fro.
Mixed paths across to follow,
lives non-fulfilment he had come to know.

An aeon passes, sequences of chest pains.
The wafting smell of antiseptic,
a term of existence riding on the success of one aim.

Grasping a ticket to the celestial city,
the giving of a tormented last breath.
The second coming of one's soul,
descending upon the angel of death.

<u>Gallipoli</u>

They were branded as brave men,
as they sailed from the shore.
Fighting for Australia,
to eventually lose half or more.

Running for the land,
a mistake by British head.
Running for a countries glory,
past their mates on the ground dying
or who were already dead.

The stench of the bodies wafted,
as screams sounded near and fro.
My mind still clinging to vivid images,
that I won't be able to let go.

Those bloody Turks were on the hill,
as we hopelessly advanced.
They were like a fearless cobra,
instance, ready for the kill.

I was lying in a trench,
as a flare rocketed high.
Thoughts were running deep and fast,
as the whistle called us to the line.

Lights blazed and gunfire cracked,
as bodies fell in helpless motion.
We fought on ground won and lost,
Until the order was given to fall back across the ocean.

For those who survived,
that battle was not their last.
For one day a year,
their mind relives the past.

<u>The Lost Romantics</u>

The cherry blossom drops,
the sun slips the grasp of the clouds.
The stream slowly flows past,
the singing of the birds suddenly stops.

I led her by the land,
down to the water's edge.
I looked her in the eye,
her hair gleaming under the blue sky.

My heart started to pound,
as I whispered in her ear.
I love you, as arms embraced,
lying on the ground.

Hours passed, the day started to die,
the cold winds taking over.
Blackness started to cloak the sky,
water droplets coming to rest on the clover.

The moon was out, the stars were bright,
the orange glow and the crackling of the fire.
Cuddling underneath a blanket,
to quench one bodies desire.

The Baby Harp Seal

Gelid arctic winds sweep the ice,
shifting icebergs pulverise together.
Sounds of scraping particles disintegrate,
a howling whistle swirls to that of frigid weather.

Her brown head peers up through an opening in the ice,
water beading down over her soft eyes.
She looks for a safe haven of deliverance,
to bear of what is hers and nature's prize.

Labour climaxes to the cries of birth,
exhausted she turns to her newborn pup.
Carefully she prods him with her nose,
and with the motion, his eyelids open up.

An unfamiliar sound turns her head towards the horizon,
a stream of dark smoke billowed from its source.
The grinding teeth of the breaker ate all in its path,
a monster of tyranny that showed no remorse.

Gargantuan men exited the vessel of terror,
in search of the Canadian harp seal.
Diamonds and pearls couldn't satisfy women of aristocracy,
it was snow white fur that tended to be on appeal.

She found herself defending a mother's pride,
although barking and charging did not prevail.
In a land of cruelty, such obstacles are discarded,
one bullet and she were doomed to fail.

Sad tears rolled from eyes of despair,
he could only watch and wait for his termination.
Outstretched paws pleading for mercy,
as the bags filled with this horrific decoration.

Club-wielding men with accuracy of woodsmen,
have come to collect their accumulation.
Red stained scenes of slaughter on fields of white,
portrays man's descent of the Stygian depths of assassination.

<u>Your Song</u>

Sorry seems to be the hardest word to say
but please don't go breaking my heart, sad songs
enter my head like boarding passengers but I'm
still standing.

It's a part time love, but I don't wanna go on with you like that.
Sometimes I think it's easier to walk away then make the sacrifice
but I guess that's why they call it the blues.

(Title references to songs by Elton John)

<u>The Masterpiece</u>

Thy am my own masterpiece,
bewildered in a sense thou not lacking audacity.
Thy pen as my confidant,
flawlessness, as portrayed below, is my purity.

Thy shall overcome my boundaries and limitations,
like a seedling pushing through the layers of soil.
To break through the earth's crust.
My existence shall grow above all that compete at my side,
thus I will claim my prize.
The utmost golden rays of life shall adorn upon me.

The Piping Tunes of The Forest

The forest had a peaceful serenity to it as the sun set against the horizon,
the crickets articulated their chirps to drown the now subdued birds.
Mosquitoes clocked in as the flies were clocking out,
an immense glow of green entwined itself through the trees that were
beyond words.

The blackened sky highlighted only by the moon and its children,
reflected from the antlers of a mysterious being.
The woods shadows seemed to swallow all sense of reality,
for if present witnesses eyes would be sworn in disbelief of seeing.

In the distance, the bellowing cries of the hunt of the hounds drew
nearer,
drawn by the sense of what was questionable of being reality or fiction.
Following a scent that no mortal sense could register,
they pursued a potential victim across a landscape of rough distinction.

All of the commotions of this cryptic occurrence centred around a gap
in time,
was it here or was it really there, only the soft tunes of the pipes would
lead.
They would lead lost and lonely souls into this forest of dreams,
and maybe would appear to them only to flee from the approaching
breed.

The mysterious forms that the creature of the woods portrayed was numerous,

he appeared as a man like a figure, a goat, a mixture of these but mostly as a gazelle.

A huge buck that in flight bounded so high tales were told of him sailing the moon,

myths of which and others were passed from generation to generation to tell.

These myths were what the town of Delta was founded on,

established for over a hundred and fifty years.

Montgomery Walker, an explorer of the Tasmanian wilderness,

discovered Utopia, an untapped Shangri-La that dispelled all his beliefs and fears.

He returned to the mainland to report his discovery to his wife,

but instead, he set about to create his own self-supporting community.

A year later he'd enticed fifteen families to build and call Delta home,

a worshipping mass devoted to the mystery that seemed to bond a unique unity.

Remnants of the original Walker family still existed in the tiny village,

although now a grey presence was far outweighing in the balance of the population.

The nights birth would see the ageing migrate towards their sacred site,

in ritual, a calling would be placed to the mystery of their asphyxiation.

A glowing scene of festivity appeared around the climbing blaze,
break away amber's seemed to reach for the stars above.
As silhouetted figures cowered in sense of a distant presence,
the virgin was given as a sacrifice for the return of his protection and
love.

From behind the sacrificial stone, he appeared, the gazelle of the night,
a cloud of whirling mist and spirits surrounded him as his body would
transform.
His upper body grew over the submitting virgin as his lower was
remoulded,
a man with deep black eyes and razor teeth swooped upon as if he was a
storm.

Cries of terror withdrew from her now bloodied mouth as chants were
sounded aloft,
his body eager to quench his desire and to fulfil his sustenance hovered.
Lives presence had now escaped his night's memento,
as distant sounds of the pack, approaching seemed to have him
bothered.

Instantly his body seized the moment to transform back to the gazelle,
and in one motion four strongly balanced legs bounded off into the
weald.
The people of Delta intern made way back to the village as fear gripped
the knowing,
that the hunt had the scent of the mystery's movements in the occults
field.

All that was present when the pack of darkness arrived at the sacred site, was the vessel of life-giving essence that was prostrate upon the stone. The pack turned towards the village before picking up the scent again, into the forest, they pursued, later to return to feast on the remains of bone.

The night had cast an eerie feeling that swelled amongst the forest and plains,
like a witch with broomstick dropping spells that land upon.
The morning's birth wasn't far from its first magical spurn,
as the drapes of darkness were drawn aside the kingdom of light was to respond.

The day's activity in the surrounds was very much tranquil to its nights, townsfolk were scarce in this pastel backdrop of a beautiful landscape canvas.
Light winds blew down the valley towards and past the sleepy village, the silence, broken only occasionally by distant pipes that captured its universe.

The mystery's devilish compositions entered the minds of the letting, capturing a reborn spirit that expelled itself from its concubine.
Sweet and healing tunes swept the land like a singing doctor on house calls,
yet it was this miracle spirit that led the ageing disciples to their holy shrine.

Day that was a lull in this theatre's production was coming to a close,
a kill seemed to be riding on the notes of the pipes tonight.
A kill that so emanated yet so vague, a striking plague or was it not,
the pack of death whom would consume upon the piper with delight.

Meanwhile, a petite but plain lass had been lassoed by the magical pipes,
she was drawn by the sweet melodies from the road into forest's doom.
Carefully she tread as branches scratched her delicate skin, further in she roamed,
droplets of blood rolled her cheeks as she was led like by a butler to a room.

The clone's occult insanities sent them once more to the sacred site of worship,
each with a fire touch in hand lighting the way.
Music of such divine quality that teased the cooling air of the darkening night,
seemed to come from the stone, the destination of those led astray.

The girl just passed the clearing reaching the stone when she fell into view,
she sensed fear as flames of terror closed on her from the field's right.
A chilling wind, the spell was broken when shackles tightened sharp,
upon the stone, the occult's cry, would she be another victim of the night?

Fire raged, illuminating the field as figures danced around the site,
screams bellowed as the light shimmered on her young naked figure.
A black mass was seen roaming the bottom paddocks towards their offering,
yet this mass was not the desired recipient as fingers tensed upon their trigger.

Shots rang throughout the valley as the projectiles seemed to pierce their targets,
the villagers turned to run realising their attempts were failing.
She turned her head to see a hoard of savage dogs slowly approaching,
their interest centred on her vulnerability yet ignoring the figure high, sailing.

As the past legends were told, the mystery swooped earthward from the moon,
was this to fight for his sacrifice or confront his dreaded foe.
He gave an almost like Scottish Highlander battle cry as he made for the pack,
yet the disorientated girl could make her saviour, his shape she did not know.

His body hovered over his enemy creating confusion and disarray,
antlers that protruded from his skull jabbed at the defending hounds.
One by one, they seemed to cower, submitting to the mystery's power,
then to retreat from the sacred and now bloody ground.

In retreat, it was known that the pack frighten easy but will return,
the mystery transformed himself into a figure of a strong masculine man.
He approached the unconscious woman prostrate on the stone,
the chains of repression were released knowing the return of the clan.

Placing the pipes to his lips he began to play, the tunes lifting her into
the air,
a spellbinding mist surrounding her entered her body releasing her of her
coma.
She returned to earth in the embrace of the mystery's arms to flee into
the forest,
for the pack to return some day in chase of the mystery on the scent of
its aroma.

At That Moment

Raindrops clinging to the window,
one by one losing life as they fall.
Neon blinks, smoke fills the shallow humid room,
the touch of a lip, a showers pouring steam.
Inch long nails softly gouging the flesh,
remnants of a once forgotten dream.

The cloak of darkness was swept aside,
satin rays ascending into skies.
Black lace and brown hair, a clip of a button,
material reveals of what is pride.
A caressing breeze parts the haze,
to upon the slender timeless body, I gaze.

Breasts so rounded and smooth,
the first chilling touch.
A misty spiralling haze seemingly growing darker clouds my mind,
a moment passes as a sound pierces the time.

The chain reaction started, as intense pressures controlled our
destinies,
the downward thrusting motion getting faster.
An alarm is raised, to awake at nine,
why one has to be a dream, I'm still amazed.

A Turquoise Silhouette

Seasonal winds have changed,
caressing musical sounds lament.
Whaling boats set sail,
mortally wounding whales in torment.

Extending far downwards into the turquoise painting,
unfettered they migrate by season.
Swimming with warming currents,
for parturition, this is the reason.

Fascination of these creatures,
have told a story or two.
Nearly defunct for valuable cosmetics,
a fight against the Japanese, a fight for me and you.

Ardour Mist

Through the deep mystic wonder of lives interlude
of love trips, one can incautiously get entangled
in the fine manicured grooves of the most bewildering
sensations that has ever shook the much diverse of emotions.

The Electronic Media

Death reigns supreme on the nightly news,
I try to change, channel after channel, it's all the same.
Conflict and cruelty interrupted only by the insensitive marketeers,
buy, sell, buy but wait I know you want more, is this all a game.

Thank God for the toilet or the coffee percolator,
I switch off, but impulses tell me to switch on again.
Politicians promise this and new treaties promise that,
a new world order they say, sure, but first, we have to amend.......

Change channels and the same story yet a different viewpoint,
who cares, nothing will become of the event.
Then after all that bloodshed, bullshit and lies, "On a lighter note",
surprise, surprise it's Jana Wendt.

We have become a society built on insecurity,
while Big Brother feeds our minds with negative pollutions.
Tonight I've opted to forget about the world's problems and reclaim
myself,
I've just hired a video, although another of his mind controlling illusions.

Sexcrime Nymphia

A door slammed in crushed emotion,
plunging into a dry eye tissue box.
It's just a fantasy of once times ago,
thrust into estranged violence, fitting doors with locks.

Reminiscent of her cherry blossom pear caressed,
finger encroached by dissonance from the door.
Pupils violated by a rotation of blue,
is this the site of the infringement of the law.

Bowing to lust entranced by officer's uniform,
releasing the entombed warrior in recreation.
Love scents into air, waft and linger,
dropping to the knees for the beef injection.

Demonstration and notes were taken,
the constable departed the house of emptiness.
Frustration takes the fro in search of double A's,
to again quench her desire of fullness.

As a silhouette sheaths the sun,
she dressed to kill, to stay out late.
Cocktails and liqueurs stirred and shaken,
man or woman, her only intention is to fornicate.

As the captured prize is taken back,
precipitates unprotecting oral with juices flowing.
With her head thrust back as pinnacle approaches,
the coming of death that she's not knowing.

Aboard the last train from Transcentral,
copulating thoughts of Michelle TV.
Tears rolling from her face onto breasts,
repeating the diagnosis in her head that she's HIV.

Night Intruders

Light slowly fades as body and soul slip into the abyss,
deep but deeper still, twitch, the body turns.
A distant light surrounded by a beckoning mist,
bewilderment enters as the sleeping vision burns.

Descending further the eye of the lens comes to focus,
flashing rays of various pigmentations clear to my aspiration.
Suddenly an earshot tenor bursts above intensely,
my desideratum for this is my cursed infatuation.

A 2000 piece jigsaw puzzle to connect,
a map of life that each piece has no affiliation.
Echo's from the outer chamber nearly awake,
but only to continue hurls upon desolation.

7.30 am, "Alarm".

<u>My Family</u>

Fine moments never touch my heart more than when I enter the front door,
as faces, light with joy as their eyes meet mine,
A thankful hug of affection and a puppy at my feet,
the family that I worship, my family, my life, my shrine.

Procuring Souls

A purple haze of soup drifted slowly between the tombstones,
the light of the moon trespassed like an intruding stranger upon the mar
of mist.
Entwined into the bizarre normality of such an evening was a new
presence that lurked,
stalking on innocent prey that venture into his beckoning plot of this
demonic twist.

Cast from the hell destined fires of some Haitian witch doctor's
execration,
the souls of the undead wander civilisations wastelands awaiting to feed.
Myths of Anglo-American culture are cast to the savages of the night,
Halloween will not be the only fright night when the untainted will
bleed.

The splatter of blood oozed down the stone tablet of a once beloved
kin,
the stench of death reigned as the chill of fear cut through the cloaking
mist.
His fawning carriage silhouetted against the backdrop of the crypt of
Sullivan,
her chest cavity separated like a crab's shell, the angel of death has been
kissed.

The stains of scarlet fluids dried upon the ashen skin of the death,
his half-nakcd body covered sparingly by severed trousers and shirt.
Sunken eyes surrounded by the darkness of his soul,
like oilfield's in a desert of whitc, yet smeared with a mixture of blood
and dirt.

Doomed to traverse betwixt the known spheres of human belief,
only to hunt its prey in the darkened hours of the night.
Voodoo magic and spells cast onto people who interfere with its
followers,
and until the source of the curse is dead, the spell of tyranny is too hard
to fight.

The Glade

In the warmth of the Everglades sunset, the alligators grew restless,
the orange and purple blanket covered the darkening shades of blue and
green.
Distant white flickered the spare existence of human beings in this
unforgiving scene,
time stood still, disregarding the outside world revolving around
Greenwich mean.

Humming of wind tunnel tunes massaged the crevices of every eco-
structure,
waves lapping against the towering trunks that ascended from the depths
of the murky water,
Reptilian monsters, glorious rulers of years long past, comb the time
locked setting,
hunting the course for victuals, the unsuspecting to be taken to the
slaughter.

Landing on webbed ski's, gliding across the black liquid, the Flamingo
returns,
their colours of beauty not evident in the darkness nor the reptiles care.
A thrash of water, a few feathers and a red dilution of bodily fluids was
all that remained,
a moment passes, life continues unabated, returning to the hunt in this
game of dare.

The Poet

Anxiety and frustration have taken to the fro,
as not a word has come that he knows.
Page after page finds its resting place,
in the desk-side bin whose level continually grows.

How about sultry nights maybe full contact fights,
baby pandas, dying soldiers which shall it be.
If I don't start soon I'll be hanging Christmas lights,
or it could just be a group of children playing joyfully.

Jotting down thoughts although it's still rough,
one idea comes and one idea goes.
Sometimes I ask why I bother with this stuff,
but where I'll end not even my conscience knows.

Now I think I know what I'm doing,
hey, there's even a poem taking shape.
I'm feeling so excited even my lions are wooing,
this poetry is really a piece of cake.

Stieger's Kindlich

The blood trickled down his chin and dripped onto the white shirt that adorned his chest,
his eyes glinted from the light emanating from the lantern as he lifted his head.
Heavily the last breathe past from the lips of his quarry lying in an endless sleep,
the Munchen night held solace in its winds for the souls of the dead.

Four hundred years his existence of feeding has cast a portrait of unbridled trepidation,
yet time has never spurned his family and he separated with his maker in Berlin.
Companions would bring him the strength that pulsed in his veins so deeply,
and forbid the vampire presence in his fatherland's darkness from falling.

Piercing the jugular his fangs sank deep like a crippled cutter into her neck,
her pain turned to pleasure as her moaning broke the silence of the blackened Marienplatz.
He would return to her three times before the giving of his own blood stole her soul,
like an invasion of her body he poisoned her and other willing mortal hearts.

Night's creatures roam the world in our fables, myths, and minds,
yet could some type of creature really exist?
Many have died unexplainably over many centuries, and how did the
original story start,
the truth behind these stories seems to always disappear into the
darkness of mist.

Α Ρεπεατ Μαστερπιεχε

Τηψ αμ μψ οων μαστερπιεχε,
βεωιλδερεδ ιν α σενσε τηου νοτ λαχκινγ αυδσχιτψ.
Τηψ πεν ας μψ χονφιδαντ,
φλαωλεσσνεσσ ας πορτραψεδ βελοω ισ μψ πυριτψ.

∀Τηψ σηαλλ οϖερχομε μψ βουνδαριεσ ανδ λιμιτατιονσ,
λικε α σεεδλινγ πυσηινγ τηρουγη τηε λαψερσ οφ σοιλ.
Το βρεακ τηρουγη τηε εαρτη϶σ χρυστ.
Μψ εξισψενχε σηαλλ γρωω αβοϖε αλλ τηατ χομπετε ατ μψ σι δε,
τηυσ Ι ωιλλ χλαιμ μψ πριζε.
Τηε υτμοστ γολδεν ραψσ οφ λιφε σηαλλ αδουρν υπον με.

A Message to My Girl

From the distant shores of one's heart, a message is sent,
passionately sealed, while already waiting in anticipation for a reply.
To fly from Australia to the Ukraine,
two peoples love for the postal service they rely.

Hearts flutter as the postman arrives with joyful news,
letters filled with feelings and kisses without the lies.
Pen, in turn, meets the paper to make the return flight,
this is a romance that will have no goodbyes.

Befreiung DDR 1990

A chilling silence swept the street,
big brother keeping an evil eye.
Despondent clones that decamp,
if not autocratic, they will die.

Manslaughter that inspires exasperation,
melancholia fills the mind.
A waste of lives expiration,
faith will adorn the one that finds.

Dignity starts to shine through,
citizens amass to defect.
Stalin's smile has been swept away,
a government's policy to inject.

A countries struggle,
a countries fight.
A strive for liberation,
which was their chosen right?

A government that has been devastated,
demolishing a wall of fortification.
Tearing cries of the liberated,
this is a cause for celebration.

Existence of Shameless Minstrelsy

A silhouette encages the light that has been,
amassing hordes of ambience.
Satan's liquid entering the entombed,
minstrelsy is struck from every contrivance.

Articulate musical pitches dubbed and mixed,
blinded by the lustrous illuminations.
Synchronised cadence of aria,
clamorous rhythms entwined with consternation.

Gaseous vapours breaching an unsaturated throat,
grasping aimlessly to digest every breath.
Foreign chemical substances spurning anxiety,
to extremes adorn upon the angel of death.

Whirlpool

A tempest grew fiercely on the horizon,
spray was thrown off the forming undulation.
Neptune's world thrust into operatic pirouettes,
stalking prey, to cater for thy creation.

A crew's apprehension, the ship's hull to buckle,
inhibited attraction towards the vortex's impetus kinesis.
Entwining, glissading, gyrating,
a sea gods revenge, manifesting his genius.

Liquid gaseous vapours clog the mind,
a painted portrait of ringlet animation.
Drowning voices are quaffed by the deity,
seasonal change engulfed with no more consternation.

For All Bar One

Stirring winds part the light mist,
through the leaves and vines hanging.
Ripples on the water as ducks swim by,
scurrying to the animal kingdom's operatic planning.

Mother gives a nod to proceedings,
while pixies fly low casting a spell.
A warning to all that's evil,
as devils quickly return to hell.

Strauss's notes are floating on air,
as trumpet daffodils await the conductor's command.
Everywhere is to be seen a courting gesture,
as the geese take to waltz hand in hand.

Fireflies dazzle with light effects,
snakes slither down to the celebration.
All forest animals are gathering around,
but what's the meaning of this congregation?

I lay in watch behind the opening,
undisturbed they go on their way.
A bright aura appears as she descends,
as the mass starts in the song of happy birthday.

I couldn't believe what I was witnessing,
and the beauty of her body, well.
Bottles popped as a chorus of Koalas entertain,
their toasting Mother Nature, from what I could tell.

Feeling alone I ventured forward,
as I shouted aloft, here's the human envoy.
But all I faced was dead silence,
as Mother said, you're not welcome, Humans destroy.

Liquid Emotions

I am sitting here tonight thinking of deep sorrow that has
been hurled through my body like an intangible flame
that keeps smouldering waiting for that special someone
to re-spark that once bewildering flame that burnt so deep.

For love is what we build and grow on, to keep that flame
deep inside going, but in lives retrospect of killing and hate
that flame can not only smoulder out but grow
to such intensity that the supports give way to a flame so
extreme that it can burn and mentally torment our lives.

I myself have felt this bitterness as if a miniature fly-blown
battlefield where so many has been wounded time and time
before, goes raging on inside my real self.

Life and love are but a Ferris wheel, one minute your up
the next you're down, this keeps on a circular rotating
motion until that internal flame of hope smoulders or the intensity of
such emotions grows to such a crippling state that you just have to
get off.

<u>Moonshadow</u>

Moon rays penetrated the window during our first night together,
the white mist parted between our bodies at our first kiss.
Moonshadows frolicked and intertwined into one against the wall,
far in my mind and my heart, the Moonshadow returns to replace what I
miss.

Stages of sanity and bliss swept slowly through me,
I know that this tranquil moment was doomed to pass into the abyss,
Yet all that was to be was a promise to pass from her lips,
a promise that parted with unrealised sorrow like the parting of our kiss.

Like delving through lost chapters of a revisited novel, I ponder,
I ponder over which path that my life shall lead.
Banish the torment that this evil has cast over my existence,
yet although this torment might not be, it's this feeling that makes my
soul bleed.

Chained like a small child locked in a dark secluded airless room,
I choke, I choke until my lungs can no longer support my breathing.
Standing over me watching like a parasite of demonic evil,
her burning stares released only by her sudden leaving.

Fears of her return pumped adrenaline through me like a train through a tunnel,
yet this feeling was also diluted with love or an attraction.
Counting the days like a marooned sailor on a desert island,
I waited, I waited for a communique of her reaction.

Like a child lying in wait to see Santa Claus in the midnight hour,
I could not withstand the anxiety of the wait any longer.
Her voice seemed dull, words were spoken not with exultation,
yet this seeming departure of warmth has resolved me to feel stronger.

This novel that was once read and thrown away was temporarily reopened,
in the attempt that our moon shadows would again dance in the night.
Cast into the bookcase to collect again the dust that clouded our memories,
but remember Rebecca that our shadows could never dance without light.

<u>Incentive</u>

Keep writing, don't get bored.
Stay fresh and new and the reading
public won't get tired of you.

Forbidden Fruit

Flick, the switch turns to on,
the motor slowly warms.
Thoughts mixing churning around,
for she's as beautiful as every morning's dawn.

For so long now I've been watching,
unable to act unable to speak.
Every feeling taken in chains to the gallows,
for every day without her seems like a week.

Tortured by watching her with other men,
like an injured sportsman on the sideline.
Life has taken an obscure twist,
with every passing moment, I'm left wondering is she'll be mine.

I know that there're feelings somewhere,
but the sky's blue, the waters wet.
I'm left sitting here in hope,
but realistically it's a 500 to 1 bet.

<u>Kelran (Part 1)</u>

The immense dark clouds surged over the forbidding plains,
plains that exhorted the dangers that lay ahead.
Kelran rode across them unabated yet aware of the perils,
a recently bloodied ground splashed in red that is now only swallowing
the dead.

A figure that carried with him the expectancies of the impotent and
enslaved,
a figure that carried with him the knowledge and power to succeed.
He ventured from Apalon, over seven moons across the desert,
to the citadel of Isiserus, to rid the land of his carnage and greed.

He ventured forth into destiny that only he held the key to survival,
storm clouds had now taken command of the skies above.
Thunder and lighting striking pusillanimity into the desolate souls below,
he set foot in Isiserus's domain of the inexorable glove.

Water descended the branches and onto his face as he took refuge,
rolling off his cheeks to alight in the quagmire that was the plain.
On the horizon, he could see the fires of the castle of consternation,
throwing his torso upon the horse, he journeyed into unfolding tales and
fame.

With ghostly like intimation, the rain broke as he came to the burcaucracy of stone,
he could perceive death as he approached the cesspool of which he would intrude.
The lack of light fettered his ways yet the stench seemed to pilot him in,
he turned to see a radiant light in the hovel to which he approached with promptitude.

Vigilance impeded his journey as the light intensified revealing the dungeon ahead,
the stench grew when abruptly his step was intermitted with the feeling of suspicion.
Looking down he discovered a putrefied body in the pool at his feet,
a gasp and shifting his heart back into place he again narrowed in on the illumination.

The dungeon opened up to unveil an executioner mercilessly whipping an Apalonian serf,
Kelran crept slowly behind the sentry pulling a dagger from its sheath and slit his throat.
Without haste, he covered the serf's mouth and motioned as he released the captive,
he paused as he directed the serf to the hovel, above he could hear the moat.

Turning he sped up the craggy stairs and through the door into a colonnade,

flustered his head turned from end to end determining which door to take.

He gyrated to the south passage escaping behind a drape when the door handle turned.

when the danger had passed he was contemplating this jaunt for his own sake.

He remembered that it was Titus who appealed to him to save Princess Lani,

but he was sure that Isiserus' sorcery would thwart him before he attained the castle.

Kelran pondered, he knew that night followed day and he knew that Isiserus would show,

but perhaps he had slipped in without being detected but Isiserus knew of this hassle.

Shaking his head reality returned with a sensation of his gore rushing through his veins,

a shrill pain passed through his shoulder yet this pain was an archer's arrow well aimed.

Grasping his dagger he spun to see his attacker stoop behind a barrel in the colonnade,

the dagger released with anger piercing the archers chest yet Kelran was now maimed.

Kelran extracted the arrow clear of his shoulder knowing that he had to reach the far tower,
the Princess would not have much future now that he had made his presence felt.
Isiserus spying via his two crystal balls ordering that Kelran is arrested as he hit the table,
a detail of soldiers made haste for the east colonnade ensure their order was dealt.

The clattering shields of the guard were forewarning that peril approached,
he turned with the undoubting instinct to the direction that would lead to the tower.
The experience of many battles gave Kelran the great sense of evasion and illusion,
he may have slipped pass the guard but he was still unaware of Isiserus' power.

From afar, Titus stood on the balcony of his castle and gathered his strength,
the night air was right in Apalon to cast into winds that would carry the spell.
Raising his hands and reciting a myriad of words that seemed to behold wisdom,
a colouration of streams leapt from his hands to seek Isiserus' power to quell.

At his table Isiserus watched his guards pass the Apalonian warrior,
he lifted his head as he could sense aberrances in the still air.
Abruptly through the window came Titus' light taking hold of a crystal
ball,
shattering the looking glass on the cobble below separating the magic of
the pair.

Lighthouse Blue's

Crackling static played havoc as the weather report was broadcast,
a southerly whipped up along the reef.
Dark rolling clouds approached seemingly overflowing with thunder,
interrupting the keeper's meal of roast beef.

The sky grew darker still as if Dracula's cape covered the sky,
he exhaustedly reached his ascent to activate the light.
While the sea threw itself to kiss the tower,
meanwhile, in high seas, a crew preys to survive the night.

Spray jacket on and fighting the wind he stands watch,
the light spiralling around sending a warning.
Wet and shivering he turns to the heater,
dreaming of bed, the storm to break and morning.

The ship turned at the sight of danger,
the helmsman fighting for the wheel.
With chapped lips, his purpose has fulfilled,
he can now sit before his once warm meal.

Perplexed

Spiralling down the Stygian depths that dispel a myth of human
emotion,
my soul bleeds an unbridled desire, staining a once unadulterated heart.
Illusions of espoused apparitions cloud my drained body,
Oh, the cursed demon of torment, I cry, depart depart.

Cutting like a hot knife through butter, I walk injured,
a ballast hangs on a shoestring constantly above my head.
The path which I ensue has too many deviations,
Oh, if this existence came with a manual, these quandaries I would
shed.

Yet, like a dormant disease, I feel convalescent,
still searching, I now venture overseas.
Can it, will it present me with new opportunities to release these ties
that bind me,
though one question still roams my mind in a tease.

Alice

Thou was not the love of mine,
of slender body and hair so fine
Nor the beauty in her eye,
that makes one, such a crime.

In all my life, I have sought,
to find my love, that I may court.
And from that day, not so long ago,
things have moved, but so slow.

To salute such beauty, of my Alice,
suite for a king, to live in a palace.
For if, this is a waste of time,
innocent or guilty, this is my crime.

A New Dawn is Born

"And now to the weather", pipes from the television's speaker,
Ken's life tomorrow will be shrouded by dark clouds welling.
With the threat of thunder and storms appearing on the meter,
The chance of a change cannot be forth telling.

The distant swirl of winds and lightning approaches fast,
The crack of branches overhead, resonant the pain in my heart.
White knuckles clenching to the thought that hope would outlast,
Yet the positive outlook was gone as there was no energy to restart.

A piercing alarm interrupted the clatter of the encircling tempest,
My eyes shift towards the reddened blur before me.
The alarm roars inside my head like the drill of a dentist,
A squint returns my focus as I read the numbers in red, 5.30.

Another working day arrives and the forecast outside seems bleak,
There's been a reshuffle at work, fulfilment, god, and more new
people to meet.
Yet there is one among them a creature divine, I cannot stop the
looks I sneak,
I want to say hi but something inside denies my talking to this
womanly image so sweet.

One, Two months pass and still nothing parts from my lips,
I speculate if you've noticed me pilfering your image and storing it in my mind.
Yet from the dim light my darkened nights return like reinforcing conscripts,
I struggled for the courage to say hello and for that day's chance again I willingly rewind.

Time passes further still and Friday night drinks loom,
I manage to stop and nervously ask if you are going attend.
The reply is no and I wonder why it's not all doom and gloom,
For would I've had to courage to speak to you again, this nervousness has to come to an end.

The depressing days of the weekend pass as Monday soon arrives,
I send an email to you in the hope that you'll reply.
I walk past and drown in Jane's smile and the glint of your eyes,
I could have done this earlier, I've acted like a child and there is no answer why?

From that day moving forward, I've had a light glimmering inside me,
My nights don't seem so wrecked, twisted and torn.
I wanted you as a friend but my feelings are more and even greater they can be,
It is you Jane that gives me light and with it, a new dawn is born.

My dreams are now clear, no more darkened storms that I fear,
You are the first, last and all the in between thoughts of my day.
Just like Heaven sounds in the background to all that I hold dear,
Runaway with me and let's take our chances on what may.

Dionaea Muscipula

To a land, that time has forgotten,
a humid quagmire that dispels safety.
Animate existence from moment to moment is survival,
where predators become the prey, this is the other side of crazy.

The life of a landscaped statue remains inactive,
mist entwining the chartreuse protracted jaws of expiration.
An insect circles with ignorance,
a gliding sustenance on landing full of hesitation.

The descending triggers the carnivorous doors to seal,
uncertainty eluded the creature to finally capitulate.
Subject to severe pain limbs are crushed,
converted into an absorbable form thus to desiccate.

The life of a quagmire statue remains inactive,
thus the pushing of a new mouth from the ground is rebirth.
Waiting for sustenance in a world of immersed futures,
another link in the food chain depending upon this earth.

Kelran (Part 2)

Back in the dominion of Apalon, Titus fell in exhaustion,
his power to intervene in Isiserus's evil plot failed.
Yet unknowing peril was to befall the Apalonian leader,
he could only have faith that Kelran's plight had prevailed.

To north, only three moons away Khepra's armies amassed,
he in alliance with Isiserus planned to rape and pillage Apalon.
The peaceful city was unaware of the danger that lurked on its
borders,
Khepra's vision was to take Apalon and the throne for himself to rule
upon.

Inside Isiserus's citadel, Kelran was preparing for the extrication,
the soldiers were combing the stone structure to run the elusive
intruder in.
The deranged sorcerer was trying to keep a balance between his
priorities,
yet Kelran knew that besides saving Lani, he'd have to kill this
demonic sin.

Khepra was the ruler of Delphinia, a barred and harsh land to
Apalon's north,
their armies were rarely defeated as they lived in a Spartan society.
The male's life was centred on the duties of a warrior,
worshipping sword and shield rather than a heavenly deity.

The army was one moon's march from Titus's domain,
when an Apalonian scout on horseback came galloping through the gates.
Gasping for breath he gave his communique of the advancing army,
the cities defences set, Titus ponders, he sits and waits.

A Portrait of Boredom

Tick tock, tick tock, the hands are slowly winding like pilgrims on an unquenchable search,
thoughts rush about with wild emotion but alas my dear friend as nothing proves to bear fruit.
Anxiety pushes the mind to a point of unstained insanity, what shall we do,
No, yes, no, yes, we look around, what, as we slide into self-dispute.

Controlled by the strings of a puppeteer our bodies continually move from one position to another,
tossed about like a helmsman at the wheel of a wooden frigate lost in a storm, we deliberate.
We ponder as to what, what we shall do? Does anyone have any suggestions?
my brain balloon's at the thought that this boring state may make my body loll and disintegrate.

<u>Secrets of The Femme Wolf</u>

Stalking ever so cautiously with every step,
unaware of the moonlight trespassing in.
Flickering light of blue flame candles burning,
a lingerie draped wolf coming forth in sin.

Glistening reflections off satin sheets,
while the curtain drifts in the soft breeze.
Cork explosions of Moet bubbling,
sliding down palette with ease.

He falls carelessly backwards onto pillow waiting,
light heady aromas of burning incense.
Waiting for the right moment,
to take in ravenously with untamed intents.

Howling at the moon in full,
murmurs of concern behind the keyhole.
Cowering over the dismembered body,
joys of conquest over the slain soul.

Not Yet Nineteen

A forehead nodding without hindrance,
suspended in motionless animation.
The whole of the world seems lost,
entwined into mist without overall inclination.

Incubating in the realm of darkness,
wandering down a path of lonesome souls.
To find a switch, exasperation or confusion,
without a warming heart, the pain never dulls.

A piercing interference breaks the silence,
ring ring, a shifting of emotion takes place.
Tripping over enlarged barriers of the mouth,
sorry wrong number, a presence of what was is slammed back in
the suitcase.

Thoughts stirring of childhood memories,
conflicting words, the drunkenness of adult portrayal.
Tracing a birth of such wicked emotions,
the death of content and rise of betrayal.

The drawing of carpentry make,
blinding silver streak, that reveals a knife.
Dripping of acidic fluid, tension takes to the fro,
knelt on quivering knees takes his never treasured life.

An Underprivileged Psychology

Hopelessness is an inescapable misery filled by a deplorable almost horrible gut wrenched feeling that restricts the brain to elude a grasp that constricts reality, conscious of all light and freedom.

Bahamas

Coconut palms hanging over,
the long white stretch of the coast.
An alcoholic liquor stirring,
an aeon of allure, we make a toast.

Place of tranquil isolation,
a retreat to Shangri-La.
Fervent chattels, the icing of celebration,
a melodrama for this place,
the place they call the Bahamas.

Arena Warriors

The birth of new light was birth of a new day,
streams of people are drawn to the race.
Daytona was coming alive with anticipation,
would Chevrolet again be setting the pace?

Ambience filled around the proletariat in the arena,
as the chariots of thunder vibrated slowly towards the line.
Hullabaloo echoed down the straight,
the chequered pennon raised with gears on the grind.

With the release of the cloth, the machines roared,
the propelled reverberation left only sooty vapours in its presence.
With the hammer dropped the lead cars are entangled in conflict,
pressure beads from the face of the pilots as cool heads are the essence.

The race commentator's voice echoed throughout the stands,
"The lead car enters treacherous turn four, No, Oh! My God!", he
exclaimed.
"Second-placed 86 cars while drafting has rubbed the leader into the
wall",
debris hurled across the track as one by one the pilots were maimed.

Yellow pennons waved in unison around the track,
the remaining chariots collected behind the lead car.
Embers from the combustion towered from the danger zone,
sirens of emergency vehicles proceeded to the scene as drivers were
trapped in wreckage like food in a sealed jar.

The warriors of the arena had come to do battle,
two dead and five injured in the quest of a point.
One week for a contingent to regroup for the next round,
to again a track will rumble with the grind of metal and anoint.

I'm in The Front but Who's in The Back

One by one the waves smash against the hull of the raft,
the raft that sails from island to island in search of what should be.
Yet as every shore is set upon reveals a desolate Shangri-La,
striking another blow in one's mind of this cruel reality.

A toy is what one's mind is, a toy I tell you,
Why was my oasis not on these desolate shores?
A question that I cannot answer, so I board my raft in search of,
a solution to my question I seek for this is my God forsaken cause.

Journeying the seas fogs and rains, enduring all the heartache and pain,
the blood drips, drips, drips onto the varnished floor and what for.
Valleys and peaks are the cycles I'm constantly reminded of,
yet we roam aimlessly around lives map unknowingly wanting to find
more.

More of what, one day cower to the sword or be the person with the
sword,
in which direction should we travel north, south, east or maybe west.
Advice threw like well-aimed spears penetrating my mind,
well, tell me, which way should we go since you know best.

Maybe I booked a return pass, I'll just take a moment to check,
but again my fears are all but reassured, a one-way ticket.
This feeling I get is like looking to the sun, I'm blinded,
someone remind me to cut this downward growing thicket.

It seems that we all parade naked covered only by thread,
and only winning the lotto would be now our lives only reviver.
A buoyancy to steady the rocking ship,
misguided we're at the wheel and while Life, really is the back seat
driver.

Carmel, my Creme Caramel

Lost in society's wilderness of expectations or may it be a brilliant charade,
she's in search of her childhood fantasy and dream.
Away from her usual trick of the trade, that of what she's made,
a desire to be floating in a bath of strawberries and cream.

A raven's streak of long locks, a raven's streak that seems to flock,
a daring persona diluted with care, that of what she will not share.
A daring persona, but is she there, oh her hands are not of the clock,
but one part of her beautiful body, no, I would not mock.

A voice that would shower with gold, a vision that I can only behold,
true feelings of this I am not told.
Alas, I am feeling weary, wait, stand straight, I must be bold,
my heart is but a puzzle and the pieces she must have, but I cannot
scold.

I wonder if I would ever be first, for this love I know there could be no
worst,
for if my soul was never struck by this curse.
My body would shrivel like a dying flower being placed in the back of a
hearse,
Is this swelling that I feel of this curse, or maybe worst, is it that she only
wanted a verse.

My feelings have been trodden, ...yes, ...she only wanted
a verse!

<u>Kelran (Part 3)</u>

The haze of the purple and orange sunset cast shadows a far,
tension thickened like a spoon stirring the pot.
Khepra's army was in sight of Apalon,
Titus's cavalry advanced in unison to a thundering trot.

Kelran skirted the pillar and into the passage that led to the western
minaret,
trusting his senses, he trod with an anticipation that he'd find his life in
peril.
It was this insight that had saved his life many times before,
advancing further he could sense the smell of something feral.

Passing a darkened passageway to his right, he stopped,
he could feel himself being watched by a pair eyes that pierced his heart.
Yet when he tried to continue, his feet were frozen, as if bolted to the
floor,
then a thundering crash as the attack had come to start.

Light beams and thunderclaps swirled abound,
as if Kelran was thrust into a twentieth-century nightclub.
All senses of what he knew to be real were cast aside,
as Kelran was to do battle with what he thought was a shrub.

One by one the plant's branches reached to take a hold of Kelran's body,
he was lifted into the air and shook about like a rag doll.
The event awoke Kelran from his trance of disbelief,
and drove his sword into the trunk and plant's victory was his to a null.

Shaken, Kelran finally reached Princess Lani's concubine,
he raised his axe and with one blow, the door swung open.
Dropping his weapon, he opened his arms to receive Lani's loving
embrace,
and his heart was dancing the waltz to the ballads of Chopin.

Dreading a reprisal from Isiserus, Kelran took Lani by his side,
and escaped before the wizard could cast another daunting spell.
They found Manisa, Kelran's horse, outside the castle's sewers,
and fled from the castle that the serfs labelled the "Bricks of Hell".

Love and War

In a world so violent,
so dark and cruel.
Nothing is now silent,
except the dripping of a blood pool.

The only love inside of me,
the purpose that makes me live,
My life that I would give,
to make the world free again.

The twenty minutes of hurrying,
before the bombs to hit.
Through the crowds scurrying,
to find my love I had missed.

First the mushroom cloud, then the silence,
then the wind and firestorm.
Followed by the ash rain,
cuddling up to a dying body to keep warm.

the horror of scorched bodies lying in the street,
a scream from the distance.
To notice, I ageing, up from the feet,
to realise I was dying from that instance.

It was the radiation from the bomb,
that aged us so dramatic.
So thanks to Uncle Tom,
the rats were in numbers, but their eating was ecstatic.

It was while I was dying,
that I went to look down the street.
I saw my love dying,
not far from my feet.

Mein Deutsche Feiertag

Paralysed in a dream,
bafflement on destinations to traverse.
To explore Australia or journey overseas,
but not to go, I couldn't think of worse.

Months of solitude to raise capital,
Europe, North America or the Caribbean.
Tickets bought and passports back,
with thoughts only on shopping and sightseeing.

Eyes stir on departure day,
boarding the crate on a great quest.
Bangkok living is the first stop over,
to Troisdorf, with Dagmar, where I'm the guest.

From country to country I see,
travelling in a foreign land with mixed expectation.
To pass through towns of carnival,
explodes through the barriers of my anticipation.

Realisation adorns that I have to depart,
shoes are worn out and money spent.
Returning to my realm of origin,
exhilarated to return but elated that I went.

<u>Photogenic</u>

Eyes adjusting to the light focus through the lens on an obscure creature,
vibrant colours streamline the plates of its outer skeleton.
Zooming closer, hairs protrude to form somewhat of an unusual landscape,
it is an insect found around the wetlands of Wellington.

Strutting down the catwalk is the princess of modelling,
an unspoken beautiful that captivates the imagination of all.
Sensuous, stylish, voluptuous, it's those legs, eyes, figure or is it clothes,
bursts of photographers bulbs light as a garment falls.

Turning into the straight the race is tight,
perspiration beads under the horse's girth reflecting in the afternoon sun.
The jockeys determination portrayed by facial expression,
bumping and jostling, fighting for the lead until the race is won.

Soaring high on updraughts the eagle scans the landscape,
a rabbit darts across the plain for a safe haven from predators above.
Launching itself towards the ground at high velocity, her wings tuck,
outstretching claws grasping a prey so volatile, with graceful flight of a dove.

Drapes drifting in the soft breeze parting the silhouetted smoke,
with the lighting correct he directs her to pose.
Make up applied and positioned on the bed,
she before addressing the camera removes her clothes.

Crouched in a ravine hidden from all creatures of the rainforest,
film captures the silent beauty of nature at work.
Water dripping off the leaves, reptiles sunning themselves on rocks,
and a curious little bower bird whom with the camera he seems to flirt.

The night's silhouette was broken by a burst of radiant colour,
screams of rockets and flares sounded overhead.
Frame by frame is filled by this vibrant intruder,
with sequences orange, blue, green and red.

The crowd hushed as the quiet sign was held aloft,
the caddy handed the pro his tool of the trade.
He approached the white projectile with intent as the pressure grew,
as his stroke rolled towards the hole, he knew he was made.

The camera was hidden among the objects collected in the corner,
as unexpected prey of film entered his domain.
Candid positions were captured on still life prints,
if some were to be discovered, he'd maybe experience some sort of pain.

The escape into seized realities locked in time was relief,
a memory chest filled with visual stimulates that tease.
Knocking at the door disrupted his journey of past experience,
as his mother requested "Dinners ready, come eat it before it's cold,
please!.

A Name – The Label for Life

Deliberation of an appellation between two soon to be parents,
shuffling through books for ideas of both genders.
A suggestion list over which he and she lament,
shrugging without expression he leans to her and surrenders.

If it's a boy, it could be Weylin, Lachlan or Quinlan,
Do you like Carlin, Newlin or Ashlin........? No, I don't think it's his callin'.
But honey, I like Phelan, Conlan and Dylan.
yet I'm able to compromise if your willin'.

I want our little girl to be Calliope, Naomi or Melanie,
do you think that any of these could be?
How about Lani, Katie, Jennie or Heidi,
They're not bad, let's go through some more and I'll see.

We've got to decide a name before it's born,
But darling wouldn't you like to have a little boy.
I can see myself playing ball with him on the lawn,
and shopping at Christmas for that special soldier toy.

Yes, but I've had my mind set on a daughter,
but the names to decide, I think we oughtta.
Restless, the name finally caught ha,
reaching out for the paper to put the list finally to the slaughter.

What would the chosen name of this child be?
she wrote the name on the paper and passed it to him not hiding her
glee.
Phoebe, Phoebe, it has a nice ring to it, yes, Phoebe,
I can see the little darling now, riding upon my knee.

But what if the little tyke is born to us as a male,
I suppose we could call him Dale.
Well, it won't be long now, you do resemble a.... a whale,
yet honey, do remember that as a family we will never fail.

The Vampires Ghost

The dirt road winded through the rolling hills,
trudging along the weary travellers came to rest.
A sign stood alone "Delta five kilometres"
reaching for the water she hitched her top partly revealing her chest.

Within the hour the sight of the small Tasmanian town came into view,
it was a town that seemed to be propelled from the past.
Anomalous surroundings hurled the travellers into a state of
disorientation,
as the townsfolk ventured forth to welcome the new members of the
cast.

Aidan and Angela hadn't time to speak before they were hurried into the
hotel,
an untamed welcome by the mayor was only forewarning for them to
leave.
He told of the six A's, vampires that roamed the town of Delta,
but to stay till morning one of you will come to grieve.

Nights silhouette started to encase the small sleepy town,
a knock at the door breaks the silence in the traveller's hotel room.
Mona Walsh the barmaid entered and closed the door behind her,
whispering to them the epilogue of the town's doom and gloom.

Six female vampires each names starting with the letter A,
find refuge in the once catholic church behind the showgrounds.
Amelia, Anna, Anastasia, Alannah, Amy, and Amber,
mothered by clone Emily and two Rottweilers known as the hell hounds.

Panic had taken hold of Angela's heart as murmurs were told,
told of how the vampires feed nightly and induct female A's into their clan.
Another knock saw the publican Col Walker whisk away Mona before another word,
words of anger piped from the descending stairwell, words from an infuriated man.

The two of them followed the voices down the stairs to the parlour,
one by one pairs of spine-tingling stares to their bodies stick.
Chilled by the atmosphere they leave for the general store,
for the purchase of garlic and to the parish for a crucifix.

Father O'Reilly was to meet them at the altar,
these vampires are not afraid of your crucifix and garlic.
These are vampire's ghosts, once immortal beings, now parading the afterlife,
the doors crashed open, "Don't believe the ramblings of an alcoholic."

I'm the local pilot here in Delta, you're not safe here,
the vampires stalk intruders people, not of this town.
Tears rolled down the cheeks of Angela's beautiful face,
impossible to portray positive emotion from the behind a frown.

Meanwhile, doors are opening and life is stirring,
able to teleport images of the foreigner's presence.
The six have expectations of a grandiose banquet,
torn human flesh and bone but blood is the essence.

The three left the parish and journeyed towards the showgrounds,
Justin lived across the road from the clock tower.
While peering eyes watched cautiously from behind closed windows,
just as the travellers reached the door, chimes from the tower marked
the hour.

Sitting down over a warm meal the lights dimmed before the house was
in darkness,
hearts were running scared in anticipation.
Justin had mysteriously escaped the darkness for the comfort of a
neighbour,
while a banging at the door conjured images of bodily violation.

The door swung open to a vacuum of mist revealing a figure of
splendour,
the sight of such beauty captivated Aidan into a trance.
She announced herself as Alannah and in soft voice urged him to follow
her,
in movements of Swan Lake, she floated away in what seemed a joyous
dance.

He followed like a lifeless zombie every step unhindered,
screams from his true love just passed him by.
Angela stood as the lights returned to their luminous state,
across the grounds he followed to the church, red eyes watching from
the window high.

Aidan entered the church and turned to face Alannah,
draped with a white cloth she shed him of his clothes entirely.
Captivated he had never seen such beauty of Alannah before,
Angela ran across the fields with the intent of saving her love solely.

He broke the spell to find himself tied to the wall,
Alannah's beauty had transformed to the evilest form imaginable.
Six configurations of gaseous vapours with bodily forms hovering above,
an intrusion downstairs proved profitable but to the vampires
intolerable.

The vampires departed the room to send for Emily to investigate,
but Angela had somehow slipped by without detection.
The ropes of repression were released by loving hands,
as they escaped by descending a downpipe to the vampires vexation.

They fled the town of Delta to never return,
the unclouded sky of morning bathed in sunshine.
Their love for each other was their key to survival,
for the parable and her rapture this was an incubus of mine.

The Illuminate Tangerine Tiger Trail

Caught in a dark forest, my mind's in jail,
for the illuminate tangerine tiger trail.
Shall I endure, shall I find, I do wail,
that from behind the trees I discover I fail.

Along the illuminate tangerine tiger trail,
I stop and glance, my thought on prevail.
Every step cracks as the twigs are so frail,
my mind remembers the hare and tortoise, cause we're as slow as a snail.

On the illuminate tangerine tiger trail,
we stop for lunch and to read the mail.
A storm brews overhead, it looks like it might hail,
and the wind sweeping the trees is quite a gale.

Following the illuminate tangerine tiger trail,
we find we're running short of the amber ale.
While darting into the woods, I glimpse the tangerine tail,
seemingly faster than a shot of an air gun's nail.

Tracking down the illuminate tangerine tiger trail,
hugging a cliff, holding on tight to the rickety rail.
Experience learnt at the world renowned Uni of Yale,
allows me to lift the mysterious surroundings of this covering vale.

We enter a clearing on the illuminate tangerine tiger trail,
encountering the huge black striped male.
Encompassing the menacing beast, our catch will fail,
along the illuminate tangerine tiger trail.

The Laugh of The Kookaburra

The rough black surface follows the guiding white lines,
soft dawn breezes parted by the occasional passing of a car.
The lonely run seems to keep going further and further,
his body injects endorphin's as the finish line seems to be too far.

The sun's early rays penetrated his flesh, warming his frostbitten skin,
and as the endless journey continued so did the battle in his mind.
The silence was broken by the laughing of kookaburra's as he passed,
yet out of this apparent humiliation, it was the courage to continue that
he'd find.

Perched high on the telephone lines above, the audience sat in
amazement,
one by one the birds joined in their laughing Mexican wave.
The runner glared at the crowd, his eyes played tricks with the visions he
saw,
as on the sideline, one turned to another saying, "He is stupid yet he is
brave".

<u>The Power Age</u>

From the far reaches of the sea,
to the land so barren and desolate.
The blood and hardship shared by you and me,
to end the war, to set us free.

To the land of France,
we came to see.
To shoot a Jerry,
before he got we.

It was in those days,
that it was great.
To kill a soldier,
and to build the hate.

But alas, thus not a celebration now,
but a struggle to survive.
Now all it takes is to push a button,
till no longer we're alive.

<u>Weddings, Celebrations or Something</u>

Pouring through the monetary drainpipes of expenditure nightmares, we spend,
dressmakers, florists, car hire, reception rooms and wedding venues.
To make all brides fantasies of the perfect day come true,
money for photographers, money for celebrants and even bloody sit-down menus.

In reality, it is all an expensive party for your guests,
an overpaid expression of love to sign that piece of paper.

<u>Traveller of The Mind</u>

Precipitation of vapour droplets rolled down the casement,
a thunderclap shook the foundation.
An illusion to traverse the globe,
to which foreign realm is deliberation.

Seated before a window,
gliding like a dove in the air.
In search of a southern terra firma,
an expectation pre-chosen with care.

Sights and sounds are graphically mixed,
drawing a feel of admiration.
Exploring lands of foreign tongue,
a mystic sense of flirtation.

The hands of time are ageing,
with every sixty beat rotation.
The world is my oyster,
I shall endure before my expiration.

The Bottle

Poison sinks
the head get
s lighter dizz
iness makes
a lover or a f
ighter poison
sinks through the veins numb
s the pains poison sinks further still the lifting
of elbows, ethanol mixes a sickly feeling anoth
er round proving a point spirits beer wine cock
tails too rotting the stomach killing brain cells
hundreds at once money to ruin health money
spent to decrease wealth what's the lure musi
c friends dancing and poison known as alcoho
l to make one sick a tormented ritual of manki
nd money drink money drink money drink all h
ungover until the bottles empty what will we do
We'll start again money drink money drink sick

<u>Strike Three – You're Out!</u>

The knife has been drawn out again and driven deep into the emotions,
on the third attempt, little Miss Rebecca has blown her chance.
It had all the signs but it was missing that No. 9 Love Potion,
she wanted it all, love, commitment, and romance.
Yet another promise to be was a smear technique like body lotion,
as the new lies and deceit started their merry little dance,
All that can be promised now is that there will be no other chance.

Simone

Beauty is in the eye of the beholder,
a magnetism that tampers with your eyes.
Incandescent rays that adorn upon,
pulchritude is the blessed prize.

Found in Bielefeld, Germany,
tenderness that mystifies.
Bilingual entwining charisma,
from one's lonely heart, he cries.

Belinda

Falling through the spiral of time,
running through the memories.
There're those special moments that you will find,
an all eternity both cruel and kind.

An image of a beautiful girl,
her hair, her eyes, the softness of her lips.
The names keep rolling back,
but Belinda, the name that seems to stick.

Stomach pains and sleepless nights,
falling into a head spin.
She contains indescribable beauty,
the heart, one day, I hope to win.

Although I told her how I felt,
after having been drinking.
Some would blame the alcohol or nothing would be
remembered,
but delicate subjects always need clear thinking.

The time is now for me to come forward,
I have been mesmerised since the first day.
To break down my personal barriers,
this is what I had to say.

Australis Australia

A turquoise mass drifting unconsciously,
swelling and stirring, lifts lifts lifts.
Hurls itself with intent,
onto the coastline lying in wait.

Parting breezes from north to south,
the laugh of a feathered friend.
Ancient song replayed and played,
for 200 years, was this the start of their end.

Operatic tunes from sails on the harbour,
a bridge with a story in the sunshine state.
A thousand cultures bound into one,
an untapped Shangri-La, is this the gate,

The weathered rock or Satan's marbles,
a red-brown land I see.
The snow is melting, the islands are waking,
the birth of a southern man to be.

From the peak of Kosciusko to the depths of the Daintree,
patriotism for the land of the free.
Splashed with green and gold,
a diggers soul may never be lost in memory.

For what this country is,
and for what it will ever be.
A future world power,
rid of careless spending economic policy.

Two hundred years as an embryo,
with mother Britain as a guide.
To leave behind all English ties,
behind the Union Jack, we will no longer hide.

A foreseen Asian attack on our shores,
we shall band together as one.
Treading out foreign dominance,
the conflict has not begun, but if it does, the story
will be told of how Australia outshone.

Futures are hard to predict,
what of Uluru, Kakadu, or the Barrier Reef.
The ozone layer, nuclear threats, or world peace,
if the path is right may there be no grief.
And if it's wrong it'll be too late for a reprieve.

Australia is for the strong,
Australia is for the free.
Its own culture, flora, fauna, and life,
Australia strives on unity, not hostility.

<u>An Uplifting Love Affair</u>

Bumping into one after another of others who were lost in time,
Wandering the corridors of life I chance.
A curiosity that captured the mind to explore further,
not expecting to encounter such an exquisite breathtaking romance.

My mind takes me back to our first meeting together,
a night that took both of us by surprise.
Neither had such an expectation before we left,
that in finding each other, a flame from ours ashes would rise.

That first interlude left me thinking,
pondering over deep thoughts of what could be.
Never before have I felt for someone like this in my life,
It's you, everything about you attracted me.

<u>Karita's Nightmare</u>

Sixteen years ago came the birth of a small girl,
unbeknown to her family she would bring apprehension.
As years went by junctures in her life changed,
denying a normal families expectation.

Doctor after doctor, year after year went by,
she dealt with a severe psychotic affliction.
Darkness had encased her soul,
then the calm turned to a paroxysm of destruction.

Covetous behaviour triggered physical rape,
a split personality, one to live, one to die.
Lethargically nails gouge tearing muscular tissue,
in a pool of blood, she'd collapse to a mothers cry.

What happened to the little girl?
such a cruel disorder slowly taking her life.
A temperament of kindness taken forever,
she committed suicide by the blade of a knife.

<u>For You</u>

Escaping the grasp of an entranced stare,
only to blink before returning.
Silhouetted by this feeling that I've got,
it's your love that I am yearning.

A promise to the, that I shall make,
to never stop loving and to never depart.
Cause if you left, this I could not bear,
as you are the closest to my heart.

Words can't describe the feeling that I have,
the beauty within you protrudes like sunshine.
Always feeling lost when I'm not with you,
knowing that we'll be wed come summer time.

Rendezvous for Lust or Escape

Under the setting of the celestial body of the heavens,
tranquil scenes lay before the fervent lovers to be.
Pulling the car to a stop before a mountain log cabin retreat,
startling the deer into the woods, searching under the welcome mat for
the key.

Drapes parted and the fireplace lit the lovers embraced,
soft breezes parted the smoke from the candles burning.
Stepping from the water's edge into the towel awaiting,
a bodily formed constellation entwined into time is disconcerting.

The birth of a new spring morning was led by robins in song,
a retreat from urban existence.
To return at the start of winter to a scene of blanketed white,
for a rendezvous de la piece a resistance.

<u>Sinnliche Begierde</u>

Paralysed by the blood of Christ,
victimised by Cupids touch.
A cursing inflammation of the heart,
angels dancing in my head.
The pain is too much.

Daggers spearing through the soul,
thoughts running wild.
Brain cells killed by ethanol,
encased by a wing of the love child.

Memories are now shot,
a surrender of the heart.
A fight, this I cannot.

Solitaire Failures of Emptiness

Wandering across mixed paths to follow,
benevolence turns to intense dejection.
A shift in environmental plates has taken place,
interdependence gives credence to preservation.

Forced barriers from vain attempts give hindrance,
that necessitate the yearn for a paramour.
Proclivity not at hand in solitary,
full comprehension is now behind locked door.

Expressive mirth bottled like Genies,
when in fact, the bottle is without substance.
Grievance has now encased the soul,
silhouette friendships cast reclusive.

No laughter, No love, only emptiness,
wanting to return to the native realm.
It's a long reach to loved ones,
with an unguided destiny at the helm.

<u>Suburban Life ...... Saturday Morning Antics</u>

The chocolate swirl dripped slowly past her cherry lipstick and around her mole,
escaped, it falls to land on her white blouse that lay in wait like a cleaners swab.
The spoon glides past rearmed with more bombs to drop before returning to the hole,
staining a moment of a garments virginity, an unsuspecting innocence to rob.

The bluebirds sing a little tune outside while sitting perched high in a tree,
the distant sounds of a rotor mower echo down the fence lines.
Wendy throws her blouse into the machine for its tarnish to be free,
the kids out the back playing war games with pretend mines.

Bob steps out of the house and raises his hand to shield the sun,
with a lead in his hand, he calls to the family dog, "Buck, Buck".
The voice of authority interrupted Little Johnny and Mary's fun,
unknowing to Bob that they were behind the garden shed having a .....

The kids had enough of their war games when Wendy called,
Bob returned from walking Buck with the paper and bread.
At the table, he read about a man who had been mauled,
and Little Johnny couldn't wait to tell his mates he'd done what they dared.

The Blue and The Grey

Two months after the first attack on Fort Sumter,
the confederates were pushing towards an easy win.
Across fields lay the bodies of fallen union soldiers,
as the South still traded in their shameful sin.

General Lee commanded a respect not too many leaders deserved,
the charge was halted outside Richmond in vain.
Tens of thousands pulled rank opposite the opposing enemy,
many to die in a valley, that yet had no name.

Bodies fell in helpless motion as cannons detonated on their positions,
could many soldiers endure the battle without a lethal laceration?
Many fighting old friends and family, they would confront,
maybe to meet once neighbourly hands behind their expiration.

A scene of green and brown was awash with blue, grey and red,
as the attack was repulsed the very next day.
Tunes of Yankee Doodle Dandy piped down the valley,
and onward following a trail of the dead grey.

The Long Hard Thirst

The sun's devastating rays penetrated the flesh drawing all moisture from
the skin,
grasping to a rail, he swallow's, yet his tongue somehow sticks to the
roof of his aperture.
His thirst is like an awakening monster stirring in the pits of his throat.
it takes control of his thoughts, his energy, his frail form takes no
composure.

The heat reflects from the corrugated iron roof sheeting for a blinding
effect,
beads of sweat trickle from his red brow to drop to the collar of his wet
shirt.
The soda machine in front of the local general store glitters like a desert
mirage,
slowly each step is more of an effort as if he was dragging an iron ball
through the dirt.

Fumbling in his pocket he searches for some loose change,
counting piece by piece in his hand, one falls to the wooden floor below.
Carefully he bends not to collapse from exhaustion to collect the
escapee,
he inserts the coins into the slot and selects Coke, anxious as the button
gives a glow.

He could hear as if in slow motion the can roll down the chute to the collection gate,

the aluminium can shot the sun back into his eyes yet he did not care.

Pulling the ring back the cold fizz sprayed onto his hand as he poured it down his throat,

a hand on his shoulder and a feminine whisper in his ear, saying, "Why don't we share!".

Times of The Tortured

Incandescent rays adorn upon,
a bubbling mass lying in wait.
Emotion chained down like an innocent peasant,
waiting to explode into tear.

A high hand with mass hovers,
with a shriek, the axe comes wielding down.
An unopened jar full of nothing,
expresses the life that I'm now leading.

Rebecca Louise Humphreys, you are it.
I hope you're satisfied with what you've caused.
A tortured soul and a battered body,
you've taken in your stride with no remorse.

Money spent is money gone,
spiralling in a six-month financial hole.
Engagement rings, the best man and groomsmen notified,
only to rectify the right you said was wrong.

Maybe selfish, maybe inconsiderate,
but it takes two baby, two to entwine.
To consider one over the other was such a crime,
but I'm told that if this was it, it was the time.

Time my fucking arse, I've thought things,
I've felt things I've never felt before.
When you think life has begun its finished,
but now I'm hesitant in committing anymore.

Let my feelings be known that I love you Rebecca,
and I always will.
You've chipped away at the stone in my heart,
but I still ask why you were so cruel.

<u>Uneducated or Not Having An Appreciation</u>

To understand is a concept that we all take for granted yet to understand verse is one's individual concept of understanding and interpreting the writer's version for themselves. If this is a concept hard to grasp than the education system that we all grew up in has failed dramatically.

You're a Paradise to Me

Melancholia fills a vast emptiness,
an enigmatic lifetime of questions.
Eternal searching for a hunger of happiness,
for the fear of what has come upon.

Pulchritude that mesmerises,
a land of Cockaigne.
Clandestine but tantalises,
escaping the grasp of despondency.

It is upon this world,
that this girl, has an inscrutable animation.
Like a puppeteer at the rains,
that not even the beauty of words holds her captivation.

Reaching for the rope of Utopia,
to be free of all desolation.
It is you, Belinda,
behind the feelings of this creation.

<u>Solicitude</u>

Joyful moments that touch the hearts,
Don't come quite that often.
A Birthday, a Grand Final win, a new love in your life.

It's moments like these that softly caress the once never pampered heart
that fills us with the utmost of glory. A torch that never fades.
But it is this light we all thrive on, love
The most divine but cruellest of emotions.

The ever present extinguisher lying in wait to
Conquer that once everlasting flame. A love so fine,
I promise to thee, the one that steals my heart.
A sheltered flame for all to see, for my passion, will always last.

For the one, I am thinking of although she might not know, I cherish
the thoughts of you and me, and hope a love will grow.

From our native shore, we will flee in search of paradise, to support that
mystic wonder that has been hurled at me. Bahama, Jamaica, the
Caribbean we will go. To kindle that I have come to know, for love is
what drives a man to the strange things they do.
The second birth of one's heart, that was solely because of you.

A German Coin has Two Sides Too!

The great depression had swept the globe,
impoverishment was vast and plenty.
A deranged Austrian had seized power,
The people's advocate he received gladly.

The voice of the Fuhrer, Adolf Hitler,
A promise to thee, he shall make.
To encroach upon Poland,
For sovereign territory, into custody, he will take.

To free our people and bring them home,
But greed and ambition had taken to the fro.
The Jews to pay for his mother's actions,
was she terrible? Only he will know.

The Untitled Verse

The deep crevice between her breasts echoed warning,
to those, like foghorns on a misty harbour night.
Colours seemed to ascend skywards from her body,
through panes of glazed silicone plates, two boys fight.

With a thundering crash, one falls without elegance,
like a toy soldier into the outer wall of her domain.
Startled her glass slips, spiralling down to meet its demise,
while its wet contents kissed softly her skin before being absorbed in
vain.

The feminine colours were now protruding an array of deep violent
patterns,
rising poetic configurations were to hug the ceiling only to be cut by the
fan.
Shattering sensations were overcome with insecurity of creatures of the
night,
a petrified morbid stare from the window broken by the passing of a
van.

An untitled street in an insignificant unknown Australian town,
beats the heart of a female living with eyes of uninvited strangers.
The aura of her sensuality now entangled by a blue flashing light.
but like charms this will not elude her from unknown dangers.

The phone ringing reminded her of a mimicking lyre bird,
pushing through her densely foliaged room, to answer may find her love.
Conversation poured from moist lips like iced tea from crystal,
reaching to turn down the wireless which amplified Brooks, Lonesome
Dove.

A ring at the door returned the emotional starved to reality,
emptiness was revealed from behind the length of security chain
stretched.
Further down the road the toy soldiers made their getaway to a safe
haven,
another time, place, or verse, the thought of, was into her mind etched.

Night after night these games of childish adolescents continued,
innocent behaviours of unknowing minds reveal.
That one's own safety and security are to be placed first,
pondering on removal to a better town that tends to be on appeal.

The Black Forest

The stillness of nothing had swept the forest,
as mother nature's pearl hung painted in the firmament.
The volume of crickets broken only occasionally by an owl,
while dew dripped off the leafs below running into a catchment.

The Moonlight seemed to encroach upon the canopy,
making the shadows reflect off the trees.
Casting an animated like figure,
moving ever so cautiously in the frigid breeze.

From the distance, the sound of chaos,
rolled towards the dark kingdom of someone's insecurity and fear.
The coach uncontrolled raced through the covered wooden bridge,
with every approaching moment, the unknown draws near.

The hooves striking against the bolts shrieked,
like thunder that echoed danger through the valley.
The coach driven by panic-stricken horses,
with fear, in their eyes, they enter the wooden alley.

Navigating their way into the forbidden forest of lost souls,
ignoring the screams of the fearful maiden.
Suddenly, deeper into the forest, they come to a jolting stop,
a stop before the glow of a lantern.

A dark figure stepped onto the road,
a tall solid stature yet not the shape of a shining hero.
The maiden alighted the coach, revealing her vulnerability,
sensing an insanity second only to Nero.

Out of the coach she feels her legs retreating,
before her, the mind could respond.
A rush of blood, pupils dilated, and her body fell,
like a wounded knight of battle to despond.

She split her forehead revealing blood,
pushing its way to the surface, like oil to the surface of the earth.
Dripping off her cheek, to the cobbles of the road,
slipping towards her imminent rebirth.

With the fall came the dimming of the stranger's light,
silence, the forest was to restore.
Only to reveal the light of a tunnel that the stranger stepped into,
revealing her maker's greetings and rapport.

<u>Something so Good</u>

Your tender touch is so revealing,

Your smile extrudes your warmest feeling.

The sparkle of your eyes radiates more brightly than a distant star,

The way you make me feel is pure bliss whether you're near or far.

This is the first of many months-years in a new chapter of our lives,

A love that is blossoming like the flowers before you.

A love that is as sweet as these chocolates too.

It has only been a short time Jane but I needed to tell you again that I love you.

Luwunu

Concealed by a craving for affection, my seat of passion is overflowing,
Jane, you're the conqueror of my heart, the key that opened my door.
A blossoming rose in the winter of my soul, for you are ever knowing,
Like a pilferer of hallowed feelings, I'll be yours forever more.

Into the night I lay in wonder, in wonder of what the future will be,
These images are clouding my mind as leaves on Cherry Blossoms no
longer weep.
Will you want to spend the future with, please? Will you marry me?
Like a murderous knife piercing my flesh my feelings too are running
deep.

Am I confused? Am I insane? For a love like this, I have no shame,
Yet I am still laying here in the wonder of what this love will bring.
You are so gorgeous, as beautiful as can be, it is you that I blame,
Fir these feelings, the freeing of my spirit, love really is a wonderful
thing.

So again, I put myself at your mercy, my lush,
As I clear my throat to let my words free.
Let's acknowledge to the world and ourselves our feelings,
With an answer of Yes as I ask you. Will you marry me?

A Letter to Jane

Words exchanged by electronic means,
The numbness of the day interrupted.
Your name on the screen beams,
Into my world, you are inducted.

Chocolate hair descending past emerald eyes,
Red strawberry lips and vanilla smile.
Such beauty cannot hide behind any disguise,
Coming to work is no longer a trial.

To be in your presence makes my heart flutter,
I cannot stay away any longer.
My walls are melting like warning butter,
As each day passes my feelings for you grow stronger.

Troubles surround our world like water lapping at the door,
I dreamt a dream of you and me together.
And those troubles seem distant and no more,
But a dream is a dream and I ponder how, how do I make this
forever.

I want you, I need you, I think I'm falling in love with you,
To hold you in my arms and whisper those words in your ear.
Yet am I a fool to think that somehow, one day you may love me
too?
My life will seem empty until into my eyes you magically appear.

A bonus excerpt from the novel

The Black Locust

1

Jane McKinnon sat cross-legged on the old worn carpet in the sunroom of her Aunt Claire's house, thumbing through her Book of Shadows. It was a day like any other for Jane—she intended on joining her aunt at the shop later to do her fair share of work as she had agreed to earlier over a breakfast of Pennyroyal Tea and lightly buttered toast. The Beltane fires would not burn for another week, and Aunt Claire would need Jane's help to get everything in order for the upcoming ritual. Jane's concentration was broken by the hoot of an owl, and she fleetingly lifted her eyes from her reading. Her Book of Shadows was a hardbound leather book, burgundy with a gold pentagram inlaid on the front cover. The book had been in Jane's possession since she was a little girl. Not long after she first moved in with her aunt, after her mother passed away, Aunt Claire had given it to her.

Jane was a very attractive girl standing five foot eight. Her lightly tanned skin matched with her long straight brunette hair of 'dark chocolate tones,' as her hairdresser would say. Her striking amber eyes possessed a slight russet tint—the family trait skipped every second generation but was said to be a sign of greatness. Her grandfather had told her once that he believed they were blessed with the ability to see into the animal world and utilise the animals" sight to foretell of events to come.

"Like an eagle," she would say.

"Yes, like an eagle," he always replied.

Jane turned towards the eastern wall of the room, which mostly consisted of glass panels that allowed the morning sun through. The simple design helped heat the house during the cold Tasmanian winters. She scanned the landscape in a vain attempt to pinpoint the source of her distraction. The owl's call, unusual for such an early time of day, interrupted the morning sounds of wrens and magpies once more. Her gaze settled on the bird perched in a wooded thicket of a nearby eucalypt.

"Merry Meet to you, my feathered friend," Jane whispered under her breath as the corners of her mouth turned upward. Jane studied the majestic creature for a moment longer before the bird waved her beak in a downward motion and pushed herself forward from the branch. Her wings lifted, and in one smooth motion, she was in the air. She faded into the distance.

Jane murmured to herself briefly before releasing the now-vacant eucalypt from her gaze. She looked down at the handwritten pages in front of her, waiting for her eyes to re-adjust to the words that stared back at her, and sighed. She studied when she found time for herself, to reflect, to find the answer for the problems that life threw at her, or to find solace in the comfort of her written word.

The Book of Shadows was the witches' diary, a collection of thoughts, spells, and rituals. The book was a witch's bible, if you will, containing the lore that a Wiccan lived and practised.

That day, however, her concentration was flawed. She knew that no matter how hard she tried, she would not be able to find the answers she sought. She closed the book, and the sunlight brought a brief smile to Jane's features as the glow reflected onto her hands from the gold leaf inlay of the pentagram on the cover.

"Tomorrow," she whispered. "Tomorrow, I will find you with the help of Cerridwen and Cernunnos to guide me in my search, this I promise to thee. Until I seek the knowledge of your pages again, blessed be, my friend."

Jane squeezed the book gently then raised the cover to her lips to kiss the Wiccan symbol before returning it to rest upon the top of the Jarrah coffee table to her right. She swung her feet from underneath her, gaining a purchase on the carpet. She stood and surveyed her surroundings. The sunroom was a converted veranda with a solid bottom wall that had been the railing before the room was closed in as a solid tongue-and-groove timber wall. Above the old height of the railings, windows reached the ceiling, allowing plenty of light to enter the room. The walls and timber frame had been painted white a couple of years ago, but Jane could still remember the smell of the fresh paint. The carpet, however, was an old green shag pile that hadn't been in vogue since the seventies. The door at the end of the sunroom led out to the secret garden where Jane loved to read underneath an old apple tree beside the pond. Opposing the door to the garden was an old fireplace constructed from round-edged river stones of pale browns and grey.

"Jane," a voice called from beyond the door to the lounge room. "Are you inside?"

"Yes, I'm here," Jane replied to her Aunt Claire as she stepped into the lounge room.

Claire, Jane's mother's older sister, was very protective of her niece, and she operated a well-respected business in town. At age forty-eight, she'd been practising Wicca for approximately thirty years and had begun teaching Jane the craft.

"Do you mind going down to the store for me? I've run out of anise, and I need some for tonight's dinner… oh, and a bunch of baby bok choy, as well," Claire said as she poked her head around the corner of the kitchen and into the lounge room.

"Yeah, sure thing. Is that all that you need?"

"Yes, it should be. I'll need some fresh ginger, as well, but I can get that from the greenhouse garden later. There's money in my purse on the bench."

"Okay, thanks. I'll just put something a bit warmer on and go. I might stop by Sophie's and see if she wants to join me. "Jane walked into the hall towards her bedroom.

"That sounds like a good idea. Say hi for me when you see her."

Moments later, Jane hopped back into the kitchen. She propped herself up against the wall as she pulled her shoe over her heel.

"The sun seems to have disappeared early this morning. Make sure that you take your coat with you."

"I will. What time are you heading into the shop?"

"About half an hour or so. I am sure people won't mind if I am ten minutes late," Claire replied with a soft laugh.

"I'm sure they won't. I'll see you in an hour or two."

"Okay, love, see you then."

Claire turned back to the bench where she was checking the ingredients for dinner. Jane stood there for a moment and regarded her aunt. Claire's features were very similar to Jane's mothers, so she could easily imagine what her mum would have looked like. Five foot six inches tall, Claire was a little stockier than Jane's mum had been, according to the pictures Jane had seen. She had brown eyes and a short black bob, which grey hairs were starting to infiltrate. The grey had never bothered Claire, though. She was happy to grow old gracefully in the company of her family, the Gods, and her customers at the shop. Jane loved her and was always thankful that Claire had taken her in. She was a second mother, really, and in moments like that, Jane imagined what her life would have been like if her mum had not passed away. She always loved sitting in the kitchen and talking for hours with Claire or helping prepare the meals, but a part of Jane always longed to know what life would have been like with her mum.

Jane turned to leave the room as Claire dumped the pots onto the bench top. The simple kitchen was a basic rectangle with benches that ran along the east side. The sink was underneath a large bay window, where small pots of assorted herbs flourished in the morning sun. The window also looked out towards the path that led to the front gate. Behind her, a rectangular oak table sat in the middle of the room. It was where everyone ate and caught up on the events happening in their lives and other news about town. The opposite side of the kitchen was occupied by the fridge, stove, and cooktop. A huge walk-in pantry separated the dining room from the kitchen. The room had a very eclectic country feel about it. Many objects decorated the room—cows, chickens, and blackboards where Claire kept many reminders. Amongst all of that were other keepsakes of the alternative lifestyle that they lived—pentagrams, chalices, and the Wiccan Rede that was printed on an old stained parchment and hung in a walnut frame.

Claire had just retrieved the last of the ingredients from the pantry when Jane called out, "Bye, Aunt Claire. I'm going now. I will see you at the shop a little later. Love you."

"Blessed be, angel," Claire replied.

The subtle metal groan of the screen doors" slow swing back to the jamb was familiar to Jane. She started along the path towards the front gate and turned back to wave to Claire, who she knew would be watching at the kitchen window.

Jane loved living at Avalon. The house had been named after the song made famous by Bryan Ferry and Roxy Music, or so she thought. In fact, she had never asked Aunt Claire why she called the house Avalon, assuming that Aunt Claire had named it. Every time Jane drank in the sight of Avalon, she felt upbeat, dreamy, and blissful. Like the song, the house was one of few things that made her truly happy. The old light-blue double-story weatherboard had white windows and trimmings and a roof of silver corrugated iron. A beautiful country house, unique in its own way, never received visitors at the front door. The house, strangely enough, faced north. However, the road that serviced the property ran along the east side of the property so that the path leading from the front gate past the kitchen actually took visitors to the back door.

Jane turned back towards the house to wave to Aunt Claire as she knew she would be watching through the window. Her aunt reciprocated and mouthed something at her, and Jane assumed that she was wishing her well. Jane made her way along the concrete path bordered by colourful snapdragons, violas, alyssum, and foxglove. Claire planted the border garden just after Ostara in September, and the blooms had exploded into vibrant colours that followed the meandering path. The temperature was starting to warm, as it was mid-October. That meant that the fires of Beltane were not far away. Jane opened the old rusted gate that was bordered by two oak trees. As it swung closed on rusty hinges, the gate's groan interrupted the peace of the garden. As Jane stepped out onto the grassed verge between the house and the street, she turned to Blue Belle, her most prized possession—well, one of them. Blue Belle was her 1971 Volkswagen Superbug Beetle. She'd bought it when she was only seventeen, using the money she had saved from working in Aunt Claire's shop and a few years of gifted money that she'd tucked away under the mattress.

She did have some money that was held in trust for her, as well, but that was part of an inheritance from her mum's estate. She would not be able to use any of those monies until after she turned twenty-one. Therefore, all of the restoration that went into Blue Belle had to come from money that she had earned herself.

She walked over to the sky-blue Beetle parked on the curb of Delta Road. At the door, she hesitated for a moment. She patted down her pockets, her fingers drawing up and bunching the material of the pocket in her palm that she squeezed to make sure that it was not there. She then checked her bag, fumbling for a moment before retrieving the grocery list Aunt Claire had given her.

"Thought I'd lost you for a moment," she said to herself under her breath. Jane replaced the list back into the centre pocket of her handbag and felt the jingle of the car keys in amongst the lipstick and eyeliner. Normally most people in town did not lock their cars, but the increasing number of tourists who either stayed in or passed through town made Jane uneasy. She wasn't an untrusting person, but she normally didn't park on the curb, and she had invested so much time and money into Blue Belle that she couldn't imagine losing her.

Jane unlocked the door and opened it. She threw her bag in the back and slid in then pulled the door shut behind her. She put the keys into the ignition then sat for a brief moment before taking the stick out of gear. She turned the key as she pressed the accelerator with her right foot. The distinctive hum of the air-cooled engine roared into life. Jane loved the sound, and she identified it her with lifestyle. She was not a hippie by any means. However, she was an environmentalist. She was a green, albeit not a political one, and because she was Wiccan, she felt a responsibility to the environment. The Beetle was economical with fewer emissions than most petrol vehicles, and it spoke volumes about Jane's character.

She let the engine warm for a moment while she turned on the stereo and checked her face and hair in the mirror. She then pushed the clutch and shifted the stick into first. Johnny Mars's upbeat jangle-pop guitar riff introduced The Smiths' *This Charming Man* before Morrissey's whimsical voice took her on a lyrical journey. The engine's hum was lost in the music, and the melody moved through Jane's body. She adjusted the vent and looked one last time at the house before driving off. She had a habit of looking at the windows in the kitchen first, just in case. If Aunt Claire was still watching, she could give one last wave. Then her gaze would follow the path down to the gate and between the two oak trees before settling on the little rectangular iron plate that hung over the white letterbox embossed the name Avalon.

Jane looked over her shoulder for any traffic and slowly pulled away from the curb. She travelled west along Delta Road into town from Avalon, which was situated on the outskirts of town and near Freycinet National Park.

She turned onto Jetty Road and pulled over in front of Sophie's house, a low-set timber cottage. The cream coloured house was accented in heritage green on the gutters, window shutters, and stairs that led to the front door. The gardens were well maintained and showed off a wide variety of flora native to Tasmania.

Jane cut the engine, stored the keys in her handbag, and unclipped the seat belt. She sometimes thought that she would like to put automatic retractable seat belts in Blue Belle as she found it cumbersome to turn to hang the seat belt buckle on the hook above her right shoulder. Then she always suppressed the dream by reminding herself that she was trying to keep Blue Belle as close as possible to factory condition, with the exception of the digital stereo that had been installed last year. She brushed her hair and checked herself in the mirror one last time. When she thought that she was presentable, she opened the door and exited the car. The door shut with a thud as Jane turned to see the curtains in the front window falling back into place.

Jane had only taken three steps towards the house when the front door swung open.

"Hey, gorgeous. How are you?"

"Hey yourself," Jane replied as she reached the bottom of the three steps that led up to the front landing and door. "I'm good, Soph. How are you?"

"Yeah, can't complain."

"Are you busy this morning?" Jane asked.

"Hmm ... depends. What are you planning?"

"Oh, nothing much, just going to get some groceries for Aunt Claire that she needs for tonight. I got to work in the store later, but I thought I'd drop in on the way and see how you are."

Sophie leaned forward as Jane approached the door and wrapped her arms around her in a comforting embrace.

"It's good to see you," Sophie said softly into Jane's ear before releasing her. "Where are we going?"

Jane regarded Sophie for a moment before replying.

Sophie Bainbridge was her best friend. They had met in primary school a couple of years before Jane's mum died and they had been practically inseparable since. Sophie was taller at 5"10, with long blonde hair and a fair complexion. She was slim in stature and looked very angelic in appearance. She did not fit into the stereotype that most nineteen-year-olds did yet her appearance was always homely. She mainly wore flats and leggings, normally black, but she would mix it up at times with some prints and on top was something that was always loose—whether that was T-shirts or jumpers, they were always two sizes too big. She was very much like Jane in many ways, but she was not drawn to Wicca the same way Jane was. Sophie had always been interested in knowing more, but she had her own path to follow. Sophie was all about connections, and she had many. Jane aside, Sophie's biggest connection was one that she rarely shared with anyone for fear of being ridiculed.

She was very spiritual and had a strong bond to the spiritual world, so strong that she could sense when spirits were near. She frequently saw apparitions and could channel their thoughts and converse with them. She didn't like to label it, though, and did not like being called a medium. If anyone asked, she gave a broad answer, saying only that she was spiritual. Jane and Sophie respected each other's beliefs, and at times, they complemented each other, especially at certain times of the year, such as Samhain.

"Hello!"

"Sorry," Jane replied as a smile crept onto her face. "I was just thinking."

"Of what?"

"Nothing." Jane paused. "Never mind, it doesn't matter... I was just going down to the shops to grab some things for tonight. Did you want to come? I was thinking about travelling over to Swansea, but I think I'll just stay local. What do you think?"

"Yeah, sounds good. Give me a sec to get changed?"

Jane followed Sophie into the house and sat down on the edge of the lounge. Her eyes scanned the room as Sophie continued down the hall, running her hands along both the timber walls of the hall to her room. Jane always felt as if she had slipped back in time when she came over to Sophie's, which was decorated in '70s retro style. The lounge that she was sitting on was a low-back Jens Risom three-seater sofa from the US. Its teak frame with polished exposed legs had a strawberry-red upholstery that covered the seats with slim cushions. To the left of the lounge, near the hallway, was a four-drawer teak Danish Lovig desk with a brown Stromberg-Carolson rotary telephone on it. Jane had never heard the phone ring, but every time she stopped over, she was tempted to call it on her mobile or pick up the handset to see if it had a dial tone. Opposite sat a huge tube television encased in a brown timber lowboy. The HMV logo of the dog and gramophone always reminded Jane of the old television that had sat in her grandfather's house prior to his death just over ten years before. What always amused her most, though, was the generic framed print of three flying wood ducks that lived on the wall where the lounge room met the dining room. Returning her gaze to the teak coffee table in front of her, Jane saw an old issue of *UK Cosmo* with frayed edges and Isla Fisher on the cover. She picked it up and started flipping through the pages. She normally did not read gossip or fashion magazines, but she knew exactly where to turn to for the readers" forums. Moments later, Sophie bounced down the hall, wearing a short summer dress and pumps accessorised with a small clutch. She stopped at the entry to the room and struck a pose: one knee slightly bent behind the other, one heel lifted off the ground, and arms outstretched with one diagonally above her head and the other pointing towards the ground.

"How do I look?" she asked as a smile beamed across her face.

"You look like you're ready to hit the town. Shopping, that is."

"Yeah, I know, right."

Both girls broke into laughter.

Jane stood up from the lounge and tossed the *Cosmo* back onto the table. "I don't know why you read those."

"It's not mine."

"Yeah, sure." Jane grinned.

"No really, it's Natasha's. She has a whole collection in her room."

"You're kidding!"

"Seriously, now let's go mole," Sophie quipped as she walked past Jane and out the door.

Sophie had an older brother, Isaac, and two younger sisters, Natasha and Stacey. Isaac was twenty-two and moved away from Delta just over three years ago when he'd accepted a position with a bank in Hobart. Both Natasha and Stacey, seventeen and fourteen respectively, were still at home. Both were very different from Sophie, and neither seemed to share Sophie's gift or have any interest in exploring if there was something in them. This disappointed Sophie but she knew that she couldn't live her sister's lives for them. Nevertheless, Sophie did hope that they would come around eventually.

Sophie's parents were still married, which was quite unusual for couples anymore. They were due to celebrate their thirtieth wedding anniversary in December, and the entire family was looking forward to it. Her dad worked the piers down at the local marina as well as the dry dock, looking after all the day-to-day and maintenance issues. He prided himself on his ability to provide for his family while doing a job that he loved. Sophie always used to mock her father at barbeques and other gatherings when he'd talk about responsibility and job satisfaction, saying, *"You can rarely find something in life that you can do and love at the same time. Whereas, most people just settle for what they can get."* In most cases, Sophie was somewhere in the background, mouthing along with her father and pulling faces.

Sophie's mum was a homemaker. The liberated woman was very opinionated, and if something or someone wasn't right, she didn't hesitate to let someone know about it. Appearances could be deceiving, though, because from the outside looking in, she seemed a typical 1950s homemaker.

Jane pulled the heavy door shut behind her, tested the handle until it latched into place correctly, and joined Sophie. They strolled down the steps onto the lawn.

"What time do you have to be at the shop?" Sophie asked.

"I'll go in about ten thirty or eleven, I think. I didn't really say a time, just that I'd get the groceries first and then come in."

"Okay, are we just going down the Esplanade?"

"Yep, climb in," Jane said as they reached Blue Belle.

2

The silver Holden Statesman cruised into the car park off the Esplanade and rolled to a stop beside the real estate. The vehicle sat for a minute, then the driver's door opened slowly, releasing a mushrooming cloud of smoke into the atmosphere.

A mysterious red figure exited the car, took two steps, and stopped to take in his surroundings.

He was wearing a pair of black shoes manufactured circa 1758. The style was known as Ligonier's after the British attack on the French Fort Ligonier in present-day Pittsburgh, Pennsylvania. The shoes were dressed with traditional square colonial military brass buckles. Two or three inches of red sock peeked out below black trousers held up by a thick leather belt of the same colour with a huge bright brass square buckle. He wore a black button-up shirt beneath a red coat that hung below his knees. His look was completed by a red Paris Beau top hat albeit slightly lighter in shade, with a small silver hat band. The ensemble really stood out against his pale, almost translucent skin tone. He carried a large cane that could have been considered a staff. Finally, there were his eyes. They were pale green, but in a certain light, the pupils sometimes appeared to be blood red.

He turned back to the vehicle, closed the driver's door, and walked behind the car, grinding the loose gravel of the car park underfoot. He reached the footpath, stopped, raised his right hand to his mouth, and took a final long drag on his cigarette. He dropped the butt and ground it out on the cement with the sole of the shoe. Looking up, he exhaled the smoke, which the mild breeze carried down the street.

The red man surveyed the street in front of him. All of the buildings were early-century timber-clad structures with covered walkways out the front. The windows of each shop were very large and well-dressed so passers-by could see into the shop to see the wares inside. The shopping precinct looked very similar to a main street that had been transported in time from the eighteen hundreds. The shops in Delta, though, were individually painted in different soft colour palettes with all the fascia, gutters, and railings painted in brilliant white.

Directly across the Esplanade from him was a pale yellow bakery, the all-white butcher, and of course the green greengrocer. The building to his left, the largest on the street, shared a car park with the Hotel Delta. The hotel had a brown-and-white German half-timbered façade that most people mistook as being Tudor in style.

He stepped out onto the pavement and turned right towards the real estate. Few people were out on the Esplanade that morning. Only the odd car drove past, and the only pedestrians he noticed were on the opposite side of the street. He walked with a hand holding his hat firm on his head and his eyes cast down towards the pavement to avoid making eye contact with anyone. Upon reaching the front window, he shuffled crab-like back and forth along the window, looking at the property listings. A strong breeze blew down the street, picking up papers and other debris. He was oblivious to the small blue Beetle that turned onto the Esplanade from Jetty Road until the hum of the air-cooled motor rose over the sounds of the breeze. He turned to see the car pass by. The driver was a young female with long black hair that was blowing in the wind. He couldn't make out any features of the second person in the car. A smirk touched the red man's features as he turned back to the window.

∞

Carla Ison was just finishing a call when she noticed a gentleman at the front of the shop, looking through the current listings. It had been a quiet day, and she was keen to get any business in that she could.

"Thank you, Mr Ashford. Yes… yes, I will get that invoice out to you today," she said petulantly, her legs bouncing up and down as she watched the man out the front. *I'd better not lose a possible sale today*, she thought.

Carla started to twist in the chair impatiently as she replied, "Yes, of course, Mr Ashford, definitely, today for sure, no problem. Okay, will do. You, too. Thank you. Talk to you soon, Mr Ashford," Carla said as she cradled the phone with a huff.

She dropped her pen onto a pile of new brochures that were due at the letterbox the following day. She checked her makeup and hair in the reflection of the computer monitor. She ran her fingers through her auburn bob then went through her checklist.

"Hair done. Lippy done," she said as she puckered her lips at her reflection. She stood and side shimmied while running her hands down her body, over her figure-hugging black dress. "Looking good, girl. Now go get him," she whispered to herself as she stepped around the side of the oak desk.

Carla watched her potential customer on the other side of the glass as she walked from her desk into the foyer of the office. He moved from one listing to the next, reading intently. She noted that he was trying to remain inconspicuous by keeping his head down and that only made her all the more curious.

Carla tapped the glass, breaking his concentration. He looked up in shock at Carla, apparently realising that his attempts to remain discreet had failed. He looked past the display cards and into the office. She motioned for him to come inside. However, he tilted his head slightly to each side, as if checking to see if he was being watched, then he turned and walked back in the direction of the car park.

"Oh, no, you don't," Carla called out as she sprinted towards the door, struggling to keep her balance on her heels. She pushed open the glass door and looked at where the man had been standing. She caught a fleeting glimpse as he turned the corner at the edge of the building.

"God, why am I having a shit month?" she questioned as she descended the two steps to the pavement. She grabbed the sides of her dress and ran as fast as her ankles would allow. "Wait, sir," she yelled at the empty walkway.

When she reached the corner, she rested her hand on the edge of the timber building while she tried to regain her composure. "Sir," she gasped, trying one last time to get his attention. She knew that her attempts were in vain, as she lifted her head to see a silver vehicle drive past her out the driveway.

3

Both Sophie and Jane were enjoying the drive into town. The windows were down, and the rush of fresh air filled the car, blowing their hair in all directions. The Smiths CD was still in the player, and when *How Soon is Now* started, Jane reached forward and turned the volume up to eight. She never went louder than that, as the sound lost clarity and started to distort. A heightened sense of anticipation built as the girls sang along. Marr's haunting tremolo guitar riff bounced throughout the car, and then in unison, Jane and Sophie turned to each other as they joined in on Morrissey's famous lyrics. Letting the melody envelop her body, Jane danced her fingers along the top of the steering wheel. She loved the classics of the eighties, especially those by British groups such as The Smiths, Joy Division, OMD, Orange Juice, the Jesus and Mary Chain, Echo and The Bunnymen, New Order, and her all-time favourite, The Cure.

The morning sun was starting to heat up, and its glare bounced off the chrome VW emblem on the hood of the car.

Sophie rested her elbow on the door and dangled her left hand flat outside the window, moving it in fluid motions up and down as she surfed the wind. She turned to Jane with an excited expression on her face. "Hey, we should just totally drop what we are doing today and go to the beach. It's so perfect today, it would be great. What do you think?" Sophie's smile reached from one side of her face to the other.

"Yeah, that would be great, but I promised Aunt Claire that I'd get the shopping done this morning and then help her out in the shop. Why don't we drop in to see her before we go back and see if we can go after lunch?" Jane pushed down the indicator lever to turn.

Sophie changed the CD to a mixed collection of '80s tracks that Jane had in the glove box. "Yeah, okay. Sounds good. I can't wait," Sophie said as she reclined in the seat.

The tick of the indicator was barely audible over Morrissey's *Every Day is Like Sunday*. The two of them rode down Jetty Road for a couple of minutes in silence, just listening to the music, lip-syncing to the lyrics, and taking in the sun while enjoying each other's company.

"You know, I could help out at the store so we could get to the beach earlier," Sophie said.

"Thanks. That would be great." Jane smiled as her hand gave a gentle rub on Sophie's right leg.

They approached the small shopping precinct of Delta known as the Esplanade after the street of the same name.

The Tasmanian Fire Service had a small firehouse on the left beside the local police station on Jetty Road. On the corner was a light pink hairdresser's shop called Little Cuts. Opposite was the Hotel Delta, and beside Little Cuts was Minty Fresh, the local clothing outlet. Many people had thought that a dentist was moving into town when the business name was hung out the front. It would have saved a lot of travel time for those who had to drive to Swansea to get their check-ups. Marilyn, the owner of Minty Fresh told the *Mercury* newspaper that the store was named after the original colour of the building, which got a bit of sprucing up prior to opening day.

Jane turned the corner into the Esplanade, where Aunt Claire's shop was located at the end of the street near Civic Park.

"Hey, look at that guy," Sophie exclaimed with amusement as she pointed across Jane's eye line towards a man outside the real estate.

"What the fudge? Watch what you're doing." Jane twisted to see past Sophie's hand but also to look over her shoulder at what or who had caught her attention.

"Did you see him?"

"No, not really," Jane replied as she straightened herself, questioning Sophie's sanity. "Why what was wrong with him?"

"Nothing, I guess. He was dressed funny. I mean, it was all olden-day stuff but funny colours. Not what you'd expect, especially in Delta."

"What was he wearing?"

"You know, the stuff that pilgrims used to wear—those funny big hats with the buckles on them and the shoes that had the buckles." Sophie paused a moment and seemed to consider what she was saying. "Okay, okay. I got it. Think of a guy dressed in bright red, looking like a cross between a leprechaun and a Pilgrim," Sophie said with a slight comic tone in her voice.

"Are you serious?" Jane asked, thinking the conversation was getting a little bizarre, as she pulled into the supermarket car park.

Then she and Sophie burst into laughter.

"Well, let's get this over and done with, shall we?" Jane said as she turned to look at the front of the store.

"What's on the list? We can take an aisle each," Soph replied as she walked to the back of the car to join her friend.

"Okay, we have to get some anise and baby bok choy."

"Okay, I'll grab that, and you can get to the shop early.

Did you want anything for lunch?" Sophie asked.

"Nah, I'm not really hungry, but I'd love chocolate milk," Jane replied.

"Okay I'll duck in and get it. Meet you in five?"

"Yeah, okay." Jane turned to walk the pavement leading around the end of the cul-de-sac.

Jane stepped onto the covered boardwalk that followed the shopfronts along both sides of the Esplanade. She passed the record store, 33-45-78, and the café, Froth n Stuff, before stopping outside the Silver Moon. As she did every time she arrived, she studied the window dressings.

Satisfied, she opened the door. A brass bell hanging at the top of the door announced her arrival.

Jane stepped into a familiar world that she loved. The shop's external walls were a light mauve colour, and the interior was a mix of purple, black, and silver. She scanned the shop for customers and Aunt Claire. The bookstand near the door displayed all the best known Wiccan authors such as Scott Cunningham, Silver Ravenwolf, Raymond Buckland, and Yasmine Galenorn. The counter that ran the length of the shop held an entire collection of valuable items: crystals, silver and pewter jewellery, swords, and athames, all under lock and key. The other side of the shop had the herbs, altar tools, candles, pentagrams, and incense. At the rear of the store were the music selections and the counter with cash register. Aunt Claire carried such artists as Medwyn Goodall, Loreena McKennitt, and Clannad.

Loreena McKennitt's *The Mummers' Dance* was playing. Jane had fond memories of the song—not only did she love it herself, but Aunt Claire always played it when Beltane was approaching. The lyrics were suggestive of primitive maypoles dressed with ribbon at springtime.

The black curtain separating the shop floor and the rear storage room slid open. A hand pushed the last inch at the top of the tabs to the end of the rod.

"Merry Meet, Jane," Aunt Claire said as she stepped through the doorway.

"Merry Meet, Aunty. Listening to *The Mummers'*

Dance again?"

"Of course. You know it's one of my favourites," Claire said with a guilty smile. "Did you get the anise that I asked for?" She walked behind the service counter in the back.

"Soph is getting it at the moment," Jane replied as she turned towards the front of the shop. "She should be back any minute. Has it been busy today?"

"A little. Two people in before ten. Did you want a cuppa?" Claire asked as she sat down behind the counter and picked up a trade catalogue.

They were silent for a couple moments. Claire sipped her coffee as she scanned new items in the supply catalogue. Jane began her routine of checking stock on the shelves, starting with the music. She slowly ambled along the racks, looking at the CDs. She picked up *The Best of Medwyn Goodall*, reviewing the song list as she turned back to Aunt Claire.

"There's a song on here called *Avalon*. Have you heard it before?"

"Yes, I love that one, as well. I can put it on for you when this is finished, if you like?" Claire said.

"Okay, sounds good." Jane walked over to the counter and rested her elbows atop the counter. "Has your house always been called Avalon?"

Claire tilted forward, placing her mug down in front of her. She regarded Jane for a moment before answering. "For as long as I can remember," she finally said. "Did you know that your mother named it? Your Daideó and Maimeó couldn't ever decide on a name. Each had a favourite, but never could they meet on a decision."

Jane could see the memories flooding Claire's mind as a smile flicked the corners of her lips, and her eyes seemed to be distant for a moment before clarity returned. "You know, your Daideó used to tell us stories of Arthurian legends. We would sit and listen to him for hours with pillows and blankets wrapped around us. One of us was always sure to nod off before he finished," Claire added with a chuckle.

"What are the Arthurian legends?

"King Arthur and the Knights of the Round Table," Claire replied.

"That doesn't sound very interesting," Jane said in a disappointed tone. "It sounds very boyish if you ask me."

"Luckily, I didn't ask." Claire laughed before adding, "Your Daideó was a very good storyteller—the best, I think. Your mum loved it when he spoke of Morgan le Fay, a sorceress. She was King Arthur's antagonist and the leader of nine sisters who lived on Avalon." "On Avalon?" Jane asked.

"Yes, on Avalon—it was an island. It was said that the great sword Excalibur was forged there and that King Arthur was taken there to recover after fighting Mordred at the Battle of Camlann. The Welsh called it Ynys Afallon. The Angles called it Avalon, and the commoners called it the Fortunate Isle or the Island of Apples. No matter who was calling it what and in what tongue it was said, it all meant the same thing."

"What was that?"

"Apples silly," Claire replied with a big grin. "And I'll tell you what," she continued, "that tree that you sit under back at home out in the garden—your mum planted that tree when we were little girls, and she did it because of the stories that used to tell us. We used to sit out there and tell our own stories, creating our own memories as if it was our own little island, and that's how the house got its name."

"Cool. So it was after the stories that Daideó told?"

"Yes but mostly after the apple tree. The stories were part of the inspiration, but being under the tree made your mum and me happy, and when Daideó and Maimeó saw that, they agreed to call the house Avalon after the apple tree."

"I've always felt at home under the tree, as well," Jane said with a smile. "It must be the connection that we all have."

"Yes." Claire reached forward and took Jane's hand. "And maybe it could be your mum looking over you, as well."

A warm rush flooded over Jane, followed by an emotional sigh. "Thanks, Aunty Claire," she replied with a smile as she stood, shedding a tear. She leaned in across the counter to give her aunt a hug, then the bell at the door broke the moment.

Sophie bounced into the shop with a bag of shopping in her right hand and flavoured milk in her left.

"Hi, guys," she said as she let the front door close behind her. "Did you miss me?" she asked as she walked towards the counter at the back of the shop. "You know how hard it..." Sophie trailed off as she seemed to realise that she had come in at the wrong time. "I'm sorry. Should I go and come back later?"

"No, don't be silly," Jane responded with a sniffle as she wiped away the tears welling in her eyes.

"Are you sure?"

"Yes, we are sure. Now come over here," she said, motioning with her hand.

"Merry Meet, Sophie. How are you going?" Aunt Claire asked as she got up from her chair to give Sophie a hug.

"I'm well. Thank you for asking. How are you?"

"Good, busy but good. You're looking well. I hear that you volunteered to do some shopping for me this morning. Did you have any trouble getting the anise or bok choy? I find the store doesn't always have it when I want it, which can be annoying."

"It was no trouble at all. They only had the bottled anise, though, nothing fresh. Is that okay?" Sophie asked.

"Yes, that's okay, dear. Thank you."

Claire took the bag from Sophie and asked if Jane didn't mind taking it home with her when she left the shop.

"Sure thing," Jane said as she got herself composed. "Okay, now what can we do to help today, Aunty Claire?"

Claire turned towards the storeroom at the back. "I've had some boxes of ritual herbs delivered that are out in the back. Do you mind getting them and putting them in the display racks, please?"

"Yeah, okay," Jane replied. "Are you ready?" she asked Sophie.

"Sure am. Let's get to it."

The two girls walked through the black curtain and into the back room.

"Is it this box near the fire extinguisher?" called Jane.

"Yes, that's it. Just make sure to put the new ones to the rear of the existing stock, please," Claire replied as she walked to the front of the shop to check street and pedestrian traffic. She had a habit of doing that several times throughout the day. The shop was doing well, and Claire made a good living. However, business was rather slow during the week. Things picked up on Saturdays when tourists and other folk drifted through town, usually on their way to get-back-to-nature treks into Freycinet National Park. The holiday season in summer was the busiest time of year, and things were just starting to pick up as Beltane and the end of October approached.

"There's not many people about town today," Claire called out to towards the back room.

"No, there's not," Jane replied as she and Sophie carried the boxes of herbs back out to the front of the shop. "Although Soph saw an interesting character before in front of the real estate as we got here."

"Really?" Claire inquired. "What was so interesting?"

"He just looked out of place, that's all. He was wearing some weird red outfit straight from some old movie or something," Sophie said as both she and Jane dropped the boxes to the floor and began sorting the bags of herbs into alphabetical order.

Claire decided to go out to grab something to eat for lunch while the girls finished stocking the display racks. "I'll be back in a moment. Are you sure I can't get either of you anything?"

"No thanks," they both replied at the same time.

"Jinx," they yelled simultaneously then broke into laughter.

"You know, I am a little hungry," Sophie said after Claire had left for the Froth n Stuff.

"Yeah, so am I, but we'll be done soon. Aunt Claire will be back, and we can grab something to eat on our way to the beach."

Fifteen minutes later, the entry bell jingled, and Claire returned from the café with a caramel latte and lamington fingers.

"Who wants some lamingtons?" she asked as she held up the bag, gently shaking it as she walked to the back counter.

"Yes, please," they both replied.

"Help yourselves when you're ready," Claire said as she put the bag on the counter.

"Cool thanks," Soph replied. The girls both got up from the floor and helped themselves to a lamington, cupping one of their hands underneath the cake to catch any of the desiccated coconut that fell off as they bit into them.

"We're just about finished," Jane said in a muffled voice, holding her hand to her mouth as she spoke with a mouthful of food. "We're thinking about going down to the beach this afternoon. Is there anything else that we can do before we go?" Jane asked.

"No, that's okay, dear. I'll be fine. Thank you for your help."

Jane returned the empty boxes to the back room. "Did you want the boxes in here, Aunty Claire?" she called out. "I can put them out the back in the industrial bin if you prefer."

"No, just out there is fine. I'll find a use for them," she replied as she walked to the doorway and pushed the black curtain aside.

Jane stretched her back after she placed the boxes in the corner then let out a slight yawn. "Okay, then, we'll make a move so I can be back early for dinner. Did you want me to start anything if I'm home before you?"

Claire seemed to pout for a moment as she thought before replying, "The pork shoulder has been thawing in the fridge today, so would you mind taking it out and cutting it for me, please?"

"Sounds interesting. What are you cooking?" Sophie asked, showing renewed interest in the conversation.

"It's going to be braised pork with anise and ginger,"

Claire replied. "Would you like to stay over for some?"

Sophie's smile disappeared as the realisation came over her. "I'd love to, but I have to babysit Natasha and Stacey tonight," she said in a sad tone.

Claire stepped over to Sophie, put her arms around her, and moved her mouth to her ear. "I'll save you some," she whispered then smiled.

"Great, thanks so much, Aunt Claire," Sophie said with a huge grin.

"Okay, grab your stuff, Soph," Jane said as she picked up her bag from behind the counter, "Let's get to the beach before we lose all of the sun."

"I'm right behind you."

"Blessed be, girls."

"Bye, Claire."

"Blessed be, Aunty Claire."

If you liked the collection or want to find out more about The Wiccan Tales series that The Black Locust is a part of, please visit Amazon, Goodreads and leave a review. Alternatively, drop me a line via my website or facebook page.

www.kenmann.net or www.facebook.com/kenmannauthor

www.ingramcontent.com/pod-product-compliance
Lightning Source LLC
Chambersburg PA
CBHW051822170626
46807CB00003B/983